A DEATH FOR A CAUSE

When Richenda takes her companion Euphemia to London promising visits to the Zoo and afternoon teas, the last thing either expect is to end up getting arrested. But some nifty action during a police raid on a suffragette march sees Euphemia dragged off to jail. Richenda, of course, manages to slip away. For once Euphemia is relieved to see her spy acquaintance Fitzroy, thinking he has come to rescue her. However, he tasks her to figure out which of the women in her cell is the murderer of a high-ranking official. This seemingly impossible task becomes all the more urgent when one of Euphemia's cell mates is slain. With Richenda and Bertram working on the outside and Euphemia trapped in a cell with a killer, they have to work this mystery out fast, before Euphemia becomes the next victim.

SPECIAL MESSAGE TO READERS

A DEATH FOR A CAUSE

A EUPHEMIA MARTINS MYSTERY

CAROLINE DUNFORD

ISIS
LARGE
PRINT

First published in Great Britain 2015
by
Accent Press Ltd

First Isis Edition
published 2019
by arrangement with
Accent Press Ltd

The moral right of the author has been asserted

The story contained within this book is a work of fiction. Names and characters are the product of the author's imagination and any resemblance to actual persons, living or dead, is entirely coincidental.

A catalogue record for this book is available
from the British Library.

ISBN 978–1–78541–658–3 (hb)
ISBN 978–1–78541–664–4 (pb)

Published by
F. A. Thorpe (Publishing)
Anstey, Leicestershire

CHAPTER
ONE

Tricky conversation over Victoria sponge cake

"I am not pregnant."

We were in the morning room when Richenda made the announcement. I had been summoned from the gardens by a maid, who told me the mistress wanted me "awful bad". I had picked up my shawl, for even here the end of summer was becoming decidedly cool, asked the maid to return my book to the library, and reluctantly left my chair set by the weeping willow.

On entering the morning room, a room Richenda favoured above all others, I saw the stout table was well laden with a mid-afternoon tea. There were elegant slices of bread and butter with their crusts neatly cut off, tiny sandwiches in which the cucumber would have been sliced so thin it shimmered like gauze, a token plate of fruit from the estate's hothouse, and three large cakes. The Victoria sponge had suffered most under Richenda's anguished onslaught.

Indeed Richenda, wife to Hans Muller, and to whom I am a paid companion, did appear to be in, as the maid had confided to me on the way through the gardens, "a bit of state".

"Did you hear me, Euphemia? I'm not pregnant!"

I did not think that such a bad thing, but it did not seem the right time to tell her so. Circumstances in the household are difficult enough. Amy, Richenda's adopted two-year-old daughter, continues her nightly terrors and arrests the sleep of the whole household. I assume the child is improving, as with each day she seems to gather more and more courage to explore her environs of the Mullers' estate, and with ever-increasing energy. Richenda still continues to insist that she must spend as much time as possible at the child's side, and while this is commendable, it is also proving foolhardy as Richenda is constantly exhausted. This is, of course, what led her to believe she might be pregnant. That she is not has struck my employer a cruel blow. She was sobbing, in a quite un-Richenda-like manner.

Amy, so the little maid further informed me, having been intercepted attempting to climb up the dining room chimney, had been handed over to my old friend Merry (a housemaid posing as temporary nursemaid, on loan from Richenda's unsavoury twin Richard) for bathing. However, Amy's loud protests over this enforced cleanliness ensured we were all still aware of her presence.

My little escort then bobbed a small curtsey, threw me a beseeching look, and fled. Yet again, it appeared the household staff were looking to me to make all things right. I felt somewhat put upon, but internally I had the grace to concede that Richenda in this state was not a job for her lady's maid, nor the housekeeper — and with Merry, a maid she had known since childhood and the only other member of staff able to take Richenda to task for her behaviour when it was very bad, occupied, that left me.

Since Amy's arrival I have ended up taking on more and more of the household's affairs. Then of course there was the unfortunate affair of the piggery.[1] Although I was away from the house for no more than a week, complete chaos had descended by the time I returned. I also had been unaccountably lethargic after that last escapade. Having witnessed first-hand the state of the survivors from the doomed *Titanic*, one might have thought that an adventure in rural England would have been just the thing, but no, I felt in lower spirits than I had done since the death of my dear father, who had expired in a dish of mutton and onions.[2] Either my mood had affected the household's, or we were all in low spirits for our own reasons.

The estate on which we all live, so superbly managed by Hans Muller and his factor, is running as smoothly as ever, but the running of the household has become almost entirely dependent on Amy's whims. This has led to Hans occasionally staying overnight in his London apartment when work was particularly pressing. Hans does have reason to travel for business, but his staying over in town because he is too busy to

---

[1] Please see my journal *A Death for King and Country*

[2] So plebeian a demise that my widowed mother is yet to forgive him.

3

return home (with, it seems, no more warning than a short message delivered to the butler over the telephone apparatus), is a new departure for the Mullers' marriage and not a welcome one.

"What if he has taken a mistress!" wailed Richenda, clutching the side of the well laden tea table for support. "I know that after his wife died . . . "

"Hush, Richenda," I said quickly, "that is not something a wife should ever consider, and certainly not discuss with a spinster!"

Richenda wiped one reddened eye with a lacy handkerchief. She is a not a woman who can cry to her advantage, being red-haired, freckled, and overly fond of cake. "Oh, you told me you grew up on a farm. You probably know the facts of life better than me!" The last words again ascended into a wail. I passed Richenda her discarded plate of light and airy Victoria sponge. In general Richenda is vastly improved by the addition of cake. To my dismay, she placed the plate back on the table untouched. "It's so unfair!" she protested. "I cannot even ask him." She gulped back tears. "I know it is unthinkable for a lady to have affairs, but that she cannot even ask her husband if he has strayed. It's all so very unequal." Richenda sighed, picked up her plate, and ingested a large forkful of cake.

I tried to gather my thoughts. Richenda is of the most recent nobility and has perhaps taken on board a rather rough mixture of morals. She is desperate to be thought refined, but has never actually been a great deal among the higher echelons and so has a

4

rather rosy vision of them. I do not.[1] By upbringing and by occupation I have learnt not to see the upper classes as my superiors. With a Vicar as a father, neither can I condone adultery, even when committed by the handsome and charming Hans Muller under very trying circumstances. I confess to sharing Richenda's suffragette sympathies, and so could not but think that what was sauce for the gander should also be sauce for the goose, as it were . . . but then I also believed marriage to be a sacred vow.

"Do you think he's having an affair?" asked Richenda, spitting crumbs across the newly upholstered chairs.

"Richenda, I know that many married men have affairs, but I cannot think it right and I also cannot believe Hans would do this to you so soon after your marriage."

"It has been an ill-fated marriage." Richenda gave an enormous sniff. "It's not as if he married me for love."

I came and sat down on the edge of a chair close to her. Richenda and I have never had the kind of relationship where we fall into each other's arms

---

[1] My mother, who ran away from her father the Earl when she fell in love with the local curate, has on more than one occasion enlightened me as to the morals of the "upper crust". Chief amongst her homilies was the "do as I say, not as I do" attitude they had towards their servants. Of course, having chosen to marry a Vicar, she always took the moral high ground and expected me to do the same.

amidst girlish exclamations of eternal friendship.[1] But I was not unfeeling towards her in her distress.

"Richenda," I said in what I hoped was a calming tone, "you and Hans arranged this marriage between you. Hans wanted an heir and you sought be to properly established away from the influence of your twin. However ... I am unsure how I can present this to you without causing further distress, but ... "

Richenda wiped her eyes on her sodden handkerchief and put down her cake plate; an indication, if ever there was one, that she was about to say something serious. "You are skirting around the fact that despite the fact Hans is half-German I was far from being his only option." She sighed. "I think you forget about my banking shares."

I shook my head so vigorously a pin flew out. "If I have learnt one thing from sharing Hans Muller's home, it is that he despises those who do not earn what they own. He is not the sort of man to live off his wife's property. It would not surprise me to learn that he is considering approaching you about leaving those shares in trust for any offspring you may have."

Richenda's jaw dropped.

"He's already asked you, hasn't he?"

---

[1] I confess I am still trying to get past the time she locked me in a cupboard with her unwashed clothes. To this day I cannot face onions at the dining table.

"Sometimes, Euphemia, I wonder if you are a witch. I mean, after all that business with Madam Arcana and you being linked to the dead . . . "[1]

"Never mind about that," I said briskly. "It was all nonsense. The important point is that Hans chose you as his wife for a reason."

Red-eyed, dishevelled, with a figure enlarged by having her own over-indulgent cook, mottled-cheeked and past the first flush of youth, Richenda looked hopefully at me. I placed my hand on one of hers. It was sticky, I could only hope with jam.

"I think," I said, willing each word to be true, "that Hans sees in you kindliness and a goodness that others may have not. I think he thought that you would make each other good companions for life, and that you would be a good mother to his children."

Richenda stood up. "I see," she said. Two words and I felt foreboding overcome me. "What you are actually saying is that any mistress is a mere diversion and that I am his for life, so I should overlook his escapade." She hissed the last word through gritted teeth. "For all I know you may be more *au blackcurrant*[2] with his situation."

She had stopped short of accusing me of being Hans's mistress myself, but not by much. The signal was clear. If I had any sense I would stop defending Hans now. And I would definitely not put into words the thought that after the frequent miscarriages of his

---

[1] See my journal *A Death in the Asylum* for further details.

[2] Richenda had never excelled at French.

ethereal first wife, Hans had chosen a wife of good English breeding stock, with suitably wide hips.[1]

"There is only one thing to be done," declared Richenda, "we must speak to Hans tonight at supper. I shall have Stone telephone his office to inform him he is required to dine at home tonight."

"I shall take supper in my room," I said quickly.

"Oh no you won't, Euphemia," said Richenda, reaching defiantly for another piece of cake, "I want you present for this conversation."

---

[1] Having lived on a farm, such thoughts can never be completely driven away. Perhaps my mother was right when she forbade me to have anything to do with our livestock.

CHAPTER
TWO

In which the butler is almost undone and I am forced to flee the room

We did not make it to supper.

I do not believe I have ever begged so hard for anything as I begged Richenda to excuse me from supper, but it was barely five o'clock when we heard the crunch of gravel under the wheels of an automobile. Later I heard Stone had only been halfway across the hall before the door flew open and Hans erupted through the front door. "Practically threw his hat at me," Stone said, "begging your pardon, miss, but I have never seen a thing like it." He coughed. He was serving me "a light refreshment" in my boudoir as dinner had been put "on hold for the present".

"In all the time I've served Mr Muller I have never known him show," and at this point Stone bit his lip, "I have never known him show," — and here his voice definitely wobbled — "*emotion* before the staff. Even in the bad days when the first Mrs Muller was still with us, he always kept himself well in hand."

"I fear he was alarmed by Mrs Muller's telegram," I said. "He must have returned fearing the worst."

"I understand that, miss, and I have never thought Mr Muller to be lacking in the sensibilities natural to a gentleman of his standing. But a hat in the face, Miss Euphemia! It is quite without precedent."

I did not make the mistake of offering to speak to Hans about the matter. I realised that it was a measure of how truly disturbed Stone was that he had even gone so far as to mention it to me. And then there was a moment, an horrific moment, when he had picked up the creamer before the teapot. Fortunately, he checked himself in time and replaced the milk jug before doing irreparable damage to his career. For such a faux pas Stone would have undoubtedly given himself notice to quit on the spot, but the moment passed. He retired back to his butler's pantry to calm his nerves and to do his best to wipe those last two hours from his mind. In some butlers this might mean liberating a part of the wine cellar, but Stone, I knew, took his consolation in polishing.

I had barely taken two sips of my tea when the gong for dinner sounded. I could imagine Stone's confusion. The poor man would not know if he was coming or going. I had already changed for dinner, and while it was unclear if this was the first or second bell, I made my way to the drawing room hoping for a little courage in the form of a small sherry.

Stone was present once more and his implacable face told me as far as he was concerned our previous conversation had not happened. I barely nodded at him as I collected my sherry from the tray he held out to me. His eyelids flickered at my cavalier treatment and I

10

sensed his assent. Our respective positions were restored.[1]

There was no one else in the room. I went to the window and drew back a heavy drape so I could watch the evening come into its full glory. We had yet to embrace the early dark nights of winter, but the shading of blues, purples, and greys across the vast expanse of sky that hung over the Muller Estate showed that twilight had already put on her evening dress and was preparing to come downstairs. Unlike my employers.

I spent a while at the window sipping my sherry. Stone appeared at my elbow to take away my empty glass and enquiring if I required another. I shook my head. With little else to do I made my way across to the piano. The lid was a little stiff. I ran my fingers across the keys. The instrument was in need of tuning, but not badly so. I played from memory some of the pieces my mother had made me practise for hours. The learning had been torture, but they were so ingrained in me by repetition that I could now play easily and with little thought. I gazed out of the window, watching the last sigh of the day and played on.

"I didn't know you could play."

Richenda's voice cut through my thoughts like the sound of a chainsaw during an afternoon picnic. I stood up quickly, closing the lid and almost trapping my fingers. "I haven't for a very long time," I said, "but it

_____

[1] I had already made a friend of one butler. Two would be going beyond folly.

seems some things never leave you. My mother was a hard taskmaster."

"Your mother?" asked Richenda.

Hans appeared behind her. "I haven't heard that instrument played since my wife died."

Richenda gave a loud snort.

"I'm so sorry, Hans," I said. "I didn't meant to bring back bad memories."

"Not at all. I shall get the instrument tuned for you. Perhaps Richenda . . .?"

"Not on your life," muttered Richenda under her breath, but aloud she said, "My talents are more on horseback than in the drawing room, my dear."

"Of course, my dear," said Hans, "whatever makes you happy."

I shivered. They were not normally the kind of couple who treated each other with open affection. Of course, Hans is the kind of man who opens doors, remembers shawls, ensures his wife always has to hand whatever trifles she might want,[1] but he and Richenda have never been a cooing couple.

"Shall we dine?" asked Richenda brightly. "As Hans came back unexpectedly I have no other guests arranged, but I am sure dining en familie will be just the thing.

"Delightful," said Hans. "You must pretend I am not here and carry on as you two normally would without my supervision." Hans's face remained unreadable, but there was something behind these words I could not

---

[1] In Richenda's case this is usually cake.

fathom. I felt my appetite disappear. I wished someone would simply tell me what was going on. I looked around for Stone, but like any good servant on the eve of a family discussion he had disappeared.

Soup was already set out at our places. It had become the latest fashion to walk into the dining room and find the first course awaiting you. I wondered how long this soup had been waiting. Fortunately it transpired to be a cold pea and mint soup. At least, I assumed it was meant to be cold.

Stone reappeared to pour wine. Hans nodded at the bottle and turned to his wife, "As you were saying, Richenda, I think life in the country . . . "

"*Pas deviant*, the servants!" exclaimed Richenda.

"My dear, we are hardly discussing a grand family secret!" Hans turned his attention to me. "Euphemia, Richenda and I have decided that after all your recent adventures, and Richenda's lack of adventure, it would do the two of you a great deal of good to spend a few days in town. Richenda has never really had the experience of sampling London life and I find myself interested to know if it is something she would enjoy."

"Hans is talking of buying a London house!" exclaimed Richenda.

Her husband flicked an annoyed gaze in her direction. "It is far from decided," he said levelly. "Whatever happens, as far as I am concerned this is the family home and where we shall be spending the majority of our time. The estate needs my attention."

"You have a factor," said Richenda.

"And excellent though he is," countered Hans, "a country estate thrives best with the family in residence." His tone was not unfriendly, but it was final.

Richenda bridled, took a hearty bite out of bread roll, and chewed aggressively. Hans ignored her and sipped at his wine. I began to wonder how I could feign some kind of mild illness.

Then Richenda swallowed. She gave Hans a blinding smile. I think that, like me, he assumed this was indigestion, because neither of us were prepared for the tone and words she poured like syrup across the room. "Of course, I perfectly understand. Whatever you wish, Hans. As your wife I will always support you."

"And I you, my dear," said Hans. A little sweat had formed across his upper lip.

"Then you will be delighted to learn Euphemia and I are indeed planning a London trip. I am writing to my chosen hotel to confirm dates this evening."

"That is excellent," said Hans, warily. "May I ask when you plan to depart?"

"It is all almost settled," said Richenda. "Do not worry. I have thought it all through and we will not need to drag you from the office. Euphemia and I can manage perfectly well alone."

One of Hans's eyebrows rose. "You do not wish me to escort you in town?"

"Oh we will be perfectly fine," said Richenda airily. "I am a married woman and Euphemia is my companion. There is no necessity for you to take time away from your office or whomever else — I mean whatever else keeps you in town."

I shot upright. "Excuse me, I feel unwell," I said and fled the room. I felt Hans's eyes on my back and I knew he felt betrayed, but there was no way I was staying to be an awkward third in the conversation Richenda was brewing.

CHAPTER
THREE

Dark hints of what is to come, but I miss them all

"Do you think Merry will be able to cope with Amy?" asked Richenda for only the fiftieth time since we boarded the train.

"I think she will be fine, but if there are any problems you left very clear instructions that you were to be sent a telegram care of the hotel. Why, we can be back at her side within a day! The speed of modern methods of communication is quite breathtaking."

"Hmm," said Richenda, pressing her face too close to the glass, "did you remember to tell cook to put the rhubarb cordial in the picnic hamper?"

"Yes, but I hardly see why we needed the hamper."

"What if the train broke down?" asked Richenda. "You may be embracing all the advancements of the modern age, but I prefer to trust my travelling to a nice quadruped with sturdy shoes."

"We will be there in a mere several hours. Railway delays are almost so rare as to be unheard of."

"Then you had better get the porter to get the hamper down. I don't want it to spoil."

"But what if we break down?" I asked archly.

"Get the porter, Euphemia," said Richenda darkly. Richenda did not appreciate merriment where her food was concerned, but at least I had diverted her away from thinking about Amy. While I was as yet unable to fathom what was going on between Hans and Richenda, and I really did not want to know, in so much as I only wanted information to stay away from dangerous conversations and situations, I did believe a few days away from the never-sleeping Amy and the confines of the Muller Estate would be good for Richenda. I pushed to the back of my mind my fear that she had some nightmarish plan of confronting Hans in London with a view to exposing his mistress.

Richenda's father had received his minor title for making his money in trade, namely arms manufacturing and running a small bank. As such Richenda had pretensions to "society", and since marrying Hans, and coming into her own inheritance, access to a great deal of money — at least by my standards. She did not, sadly, have the training or temperament to either cope with her current position nor the ability to ascend the slippery social ladder.

I could help her, of course. My mother's own training as the daughter of an Earl had more than equipped her to train me in the ways of society I was forever barred from attending. (My mother eloping with the curate, who was to become my father, had upset everyone a great deal. By which I mean she had provided goodly entertainment in smoking rooms and drawing rooms up and down the land to the extent that her mother had banned her name from every being mentioned again in her house. Fortunately she was only a girl and there were brothers to carry on the family name.) But there was only so far Richenda could be helped. She was stubborn and headstrong and although her marriage had brought out the very best in her and I knew her of good heart, I also knew that there was no way on God's green earth that she would ever be able to hold her own in a duchess' drawing room. If she had been born into a position of greatness, she would have been thought eccentric, and if noble and rich enough, "a great character". As the daughter of a banker and married to man who made his living "working" in the city — and who did not even own his bank, Richenda and her manners would see her snubbed and excluded from the society she so longed to join.

Personally, I found it most confusing. I have always found the most congenial people work below stairs, although at the Muller Estate, where I arrived as a companion, I have never mixed socially with the servants. In fact, I reflected as the porter lugged down our very large hamper, and fields of fluffy sheep flew by, in some ways I was as much a fish out of water as Richenda. I tried to think of a cheering topic of conversation, but there was no need. Cook had included a large Victoria sponge, pre-sliced, and Richenda had already descended upon it, an expression of glee on her face and all difficult matters clearly dismissed from her mind. If only I could do the same.

The train station was loud, crowded, and dirty. I had barely descended from the train and was in the midst of arranging a porter, when a smart young man in a grey, well-pressed chauffeur's uniform appeared. "Miss Euphemia? Mrs Muller? Mr Muller sent me with a car for you to take you to the hotel."

He flipped a coin at the porter and quietly bade him to "follow us, mate", before escorting us to the waiting the car. Richenda went forward to take his arm, but I nipped her ample waist. "Not done," I whispered in her ear. Her eyes went wide. "Thank you," she whispered back unexpectedly. I read in her face an uncertainty I had not seen before. Perhaps it would not be so hard to turn her from her London course and send us both back to the country. There I could show her how to be lady of the manor holding balls, dinner parties and all manner of entertainments that would feed her desire to feel important. At home she could be Queen of all she surveyed. In London, I feared she would be as little appreciated by society as the lingering smell of the stables that all too often hung about her.

The hotel was charming. The doorman looked smart enough to wait on the King himself. The railings beside the steps which led to the grand wooden doors were brightly polished, and the steps slightly more shiny than it is meant possible for stone to be. Bellboys took our luggage without being asked and loaded it onto brass trolleys. Doors were opened for us. It was made evident that we were to be allowed to breathe for ourselves, but not much more. At the desk the clerk had already been tipped as to who we were by the chauffeur, but Richenda then embarked on telling the bewildered clerk about her special needs. I cut her short.

"It would be easier, do you not think, Mrs Muller, to have the manager come to our suite?" I tried to say it as kindly as I could and the clerk jumped on the idea with alacrity. Richenda managed to assent, perhaps a touch too regally, but she exited the conversation with grace. However, I noticed the faint blush on her cheeks. It had not occurred to me that she would never have stayed in a hotel before.

Once the bellboys had deposited our luggage and promised that maids would attend us shortly to see to our unpacking, the door closed behind us, Richenda threw herself, still hatted, down into a chair. "Oh good heavens, Euphemia," she said, "you're going to have to tell me how to go on. This is all much more difficult than I imagined. And it is only a wretched hotel."

I saw her eyes were shining with unshed tears. "Let me order us some tea, while you take off your hat and change," I suggested.

"To think I almost took the chauffeur's arm," sighed Richenda, in the manner of a Duchess who has almost inadvertently mistaken Indian for China tea. "But tomorrow, you'll see, Euphemia, it will all be different. It is going to be a great day."

"What's tomorrow?" I asked, but Richenda would only answer with a sly smile. My imagination conjured up the most disturbing of possibilities, but nothing could have prepared me for what was to happen.

CHAPTER
FOUR

Unsightly apparel and brisk exercise lead us into danger

Breakfast the next morning was a splendid affair. I could almost imagine myself on one of my adventures with Bertram and Rory. Although both of them were thoroughly versed in the ways of the metropolis. "It seems inconsistent," I remarked to Richenda, "that men are expected to be well-versed in the ways of the world from their first entry into manhood, while young women are kept at home and allowed no such worldly education." As I'd hoped, my comment was greeted with a broad smile. Richenda had kept to our private suite for the rest of day on our arrival, even having our dinner sent up. She had seemed preoccupied and even forlorn, so I was glad to see her brightening. We were only in London for three days, and lovely though the hotel was, it seemed a great shame to spend all our time in it. We had no society invitations with which to fill our time, despite Richenda ringing down to the desk on the hour, every hour, yesterday. However, I did believe that it was possible to do some genteel sightseeing in this modern age. Certainly we could not join the ranks of the penny-spending day trippers, but a word with the concierge had brought me quickly up to speed with expeditions that would not be considered overly vulgar.

I had read about the reorganisation of London Zoological Gardens and Dr Mitchell's radical new concept that the animals could survive outside buildings and in open enclosures. It sounded much nicer for the animals and I was keen to see several exotic species that the Zoological Gardens maintained. I thought that in our less expensive dresses it might pass as a suitable entertainment. And of course, there were many, many theatres, some of which were visited by the cream of society. All this along with indulging in some shopping at the very best shops and taking tea in London's exquisitely elegant tearooms promised to make this a most jolly visit.[1]

"Thank you for wearing the clothes I had made up for you," said Richenda through a mouthful of hot smoked salmon. "I know you are not completely convinced these are your colours, but they are much better than that awful dress you wore at Hans's ball. (The dress had been a gift and, though I say so myself, had brought out the very best of my features.)

"I quite see that," I said equitably. Richenda has been convinced for some time now I should dress in green and purple and often buys me clothing in these colours. They make me resemble a mouldy cabbage,

---

[1] I doubt my mother would have attended any of these, but Richenda's mother was not an Earl's daughter and Richenda would have to grow accustomed to that fact. Besides, I thought we might have no little amusement from our trip.

but I know that to some people's eyes I am the prettier of the two of us and it is natural for a married woman to take steps to prevent her husband noticing the charms of any of the women in her household.[1] I had been a little surprised to see that Richenda had again set her heart on my wearing this outfit in London, but looking like decaying vegetation, I told myself, was a small price to pay for the generosity of Richenda allowing me to accompany her to the capital. After all, I was paid an excellent wage and yet the Mullers seemed determined that I should never have cause to spend a penny of it.

"I have had some thoughts of what we might do today," I began cautiously.

"No need," said Richenda, "we are going to meet up with some friends of mine this morning. All arranged."

"How nice!" I said a little bewildered. "Have I had the honour of meeting them before?"

Richenda, her mouth full of egg, shook her head. "No," she said thickly, "but you should like them. They are like you. Intelligent." She swallowed her mouthful and looked down at her plate. "You'll need good walking boots," she murmured.

"Walking boots?" I repeated.

Richenda nodded again and rose quickly from the table, leaving her toast and marmalade untouched. "Be ready in half an hour," she commanded. I regarded the

---

[1] Hans's maids follow the fashion of turning their faces to the wall if they ever encounter a male visitor. A custom and position I fear makes them most vulnerable.

untouched food with astonishment. Richenda most obviously had a plan and equally obviously it was something she felt I might disapprove of. I swallowed the last of my morning tea and tried to push down my concern at the same time. I went to put on my boots, but I felt decidedly queasy.

Richenda gave me no time for questions when we met, but ushered me quickly into the elevator where I could hardly speak before the bellboy. Once we were in the lobby she set a cracking pace out through the doors and along the road. For a woman who as far as I knew had never visited the metropolis before (except on her charity work which would have been in quite a different district), and who abhorred exercise, her actions were inexplicable. My foreboding grew. I knew Hans trusted me to keep Richenda out of trouble. I was about to catch her elbow and demand what was going on, when a most unusual sight caught my eye. As we rounded the corner into the next street, a woman in her middle years was just disappearing around the edge of the next junction. She was suitably dressed for a mature matron, in a gown whose creator had nodded to modern fashions, but had toned them down in a way that suggested both wealth and class. What was startling about the dress was that it was fashioned in purple and green with a white trim. By now I was used to Richenda's unorthodox[1] colour scheme, but that someone else should share her dubious fashion sense

---

[1] Early in our acquaintance I had entertained the idea she was colour-blind. Sadly, the truth was she had little taste.

24

seemed remarkable. I shook my head. The sun was dim this morning and I decided I must have been mistaken.

As we too took the street the matron had taken I caught sight of yet another woman dressed in similar colours, then another wearing a sash of the same. "Goodness me!" I cried to Richenda, "we positively cannot . . ."

And then on the wind snatches of a song of hope awakening, sung in the high cadence of unified female voices, reached me.

"Richenda," I blurted out, "we cannot possibly join a suffragette march!"

"Just watch me!" answered my infuriating employer, and turned a final corner. In front of us the street was filled with a column of women, five wide, some holding banners, all of them marking time and singing. If I had not been so fearful of what would happen next I would have been impressed.

Then Richenda did what I had feared the most and disappeared into the throng. My heart began to race. I agreed with much of what the suffragettes stood for, but unlike Richenda I read the daily papers. I was only too aware that, desperate and frustrated when Prime Minister Asquith had yet again torpedoed the bill for the enfranchisement of women in November 1911, some suffragettes had begun a co-ordinated series of violent attacks. It had begun with a window-smashing campaign and moved on to the destruction of telephone boxes, telephone exchanges, railway carriages, and even churches. The acknowledged head of the movement, Emmeline Pankhurst, had previously spoken out against such violence, but her daughters, in particular Christabel, appeared to be embracing it.

And the establishment had responded. The papers had carried pictures of women being manhandled by police, of women being attacked by police, and stories of the harm done by force-feeding in prisons abounded. Women of all ranks had joined the suffragette movement, and the police had shown no regard for status when capturing and imprisoning campaigners.

This might be the most peaceful of protest marches, but there was no guarantee that there were not more violent suffragettes waiting within the ranks of women, willing to do violence to make their voices heard. In fact Richenda was hardly the most peaceable of souls herself. I searched my memory to recall if Richenda had taken with her a reticule large enough to conceal a brick.

I was rather afraid she had.

I looked at the throng of women before me, cursing my stupidity at not realising why Richenda had dressed me this way. A woman bustled towards me smiling. She took me for a sister in arms. I did not protest as she took my arm to show me where I could walk in line. I had no choice. If I was to find Richenda and take her away from this, as Hans would expect, I would have to join the procession. Once we were moving I could only hope I would manage to catch sight of her and extricate her from the march before anything unfortunate occurred. I had this horrible feeling that Richenda herself would resist me with violence when I tried to remove her, but I knew the constabulary would respond in force to this protest and that when they did this march could become the most dangerous of situations.

CHAPTER
FIVE

In which I am not very ladylike

If I had not felt so endangered I believe I might have found the march uplifting. There was something stirring about seeing women of all ranks marching side by side united in their belief that women should have a say in how our country is governed and that we are more than the playthings of men. I confess I do yearn for the day that womankind will be recognised for our intelligence, allowed to take control of our own lives, and become more than creatures who are thought only to find their reason for being through marriage. As the song swelled around me I knew that my unusual upbringing, with my education from my learned father and my association with men such as Bertram Stapleford and even Fitzroy, had placed me among men who valued me, not as an equal[1] but as that "unusual" thing, a woman with a brain.

Estranged as we were from my grandfather, there was always a slight chance my brother might inherit some of the family property through the machinations of the law, but for me, as a woman, and for my mother, a widow, we had had no choice but to forge our own

---

[1] Even I am not so foolish as to believe this!

way in the world. When I left my home after my father's demise, there had been but two options open to me, to enter service or to become a fallen woman. Richard Stapleford, when I was offered employment in his house, had assumed that because I was well-spoken, I was a high-class woman of the night who for her own reasons had chosen to enter service. Even Bertram had assumed that at the best I was the illegitimate child of a man of position. (Bertram's assumption placed no blame on the man in question, though; such things happened. It meant rather that it was somehow my fault if I had indeed proved to be illegitimate.)

I shook my head. The cries of the Sisterhood were affecting me. The world might be run unfairly (and in my opinion, unwisely) by men, but the random violent actions by some suffragettes made it foolish and dangerous for any woman to join a public march.

I knew it was unfair, but I also knew we were in danger.

I glanced at the pretty young woman to my left, who was singing her heart out. I judged her to be about eighteen years of age. Her face had the pinched look of one who does not always manage to eat three meals a day, but she took pride in her appearance. Her face was scrubbed clean and her light brown hair tightly braided. Her eyes shone with, I thought, hope rather than fanaticism. She was simply dressed and obviously of the lower working classes. I surmised she was a woman who had always had to work hard and who life had no doubt treated less than fairly. She believed in this cause in the way a child of an orphanage might cling to the idea that one day their real parents might come to rescue them.

I ventured a whisper. "Do you know how long we will be marching?"

Immediately her expression turned to concern and even, I thought, fear. "No, m'um," she replied, and after that sang a little quieter. The flame-haired young woman on my other side nudged me none to gently in the ribs and stopped singing for a moment. "Emily Davidson," she said, "we will march for as long as it takes!" Then she turned away from me returned to her song, inflating her thin chest with effort, but not before I had caught the glint in her eye.

I did my best to calm myself. Who was I to think I saw the evidence of fanaticism in her face? Being part of this large throng, for the crowd snaked away into distance both before and after me, was affecting. There might well be hundreds of women here, singing. I did not have the knack of estimating a crowd like Fitzroy. It was hard to resist both the feelings of sisterhood and righteous indignation that were coming in emotional waves from the women around me. Deep breaths, I told myself, do not become hysterical. I knew this was the phrase most commonly banded about by the newspapers. I sneaked a glance at the faces on either side of me. Both were flushed with excitement. With the exercise or with fervour? I twisted my head round to look to for Richenda. The lady who had placed me so carefully in line must also have indicated a place to Richenda. Sense dictated that it could not be that far away, but it is difficult to look around when marching in formation. We were not unlike a moving version of one of my little brother's toys, dominoes. There was a sense that I struggle to describe of each of us buoying the others up, that we were more than ourselves and had become part of a greater whole. Should I stumble I feared I would disappear underneath this body of women as they marched on over me. Perhaps others too would fall, but like the ants I had seen as a child in the country, I could not shake the fantasy that the march would carry on, bodies beaten under the unison of marching boots. Perhaps I had indeed become infected by the ways of Madam Arcana, when she had first told me, that I had preternatural capabilities.[1] But whatever it was I could not shake my feeling of dread.

Richenda, I thought ruefully, would be having a grand time. She had few friends in real life, and of her family, there existed affection only between herself and her brother Bertram. Feeling as she did now, that Hans no longer desired her, I could well understand her desire to feel part of something bigger, to be welcomed into the suffragette fold, and to march shoulder to shoulder with women whom she could pretend were her sisters.

I knew I was being nasty, that these were unkind thoughts about Richenda, but I latched on to the seething annoyance inside me that she had dragged me into this mess and at my own stupidity for not realising the significance of the colours she had been dressing me in for some time. She had played me for a fool. Yes,

---

[1] See my journal *A Death in the Asylum*.

it was better to hold onto to this anger than give into the creeping fear that threatened to swallow me. I glanced sideways at Emily Davidson. Her reticule was small. Could it contain a brick? It was tied with a feminine bow, so I doubted it. If I was bringing a missile for use, I would have ensured although hidden it was also easy to access.

The noise was tremendous. Women may in general have lighter voices, but get enough of them together and they will prove to you that their lungs have as much capacity as any man's. And while men may hold this image of gentle women tripping lightly along the woman in this march took every step with decision, with pride, with determination, and their boots rang with headache-inducing rhythm.

Again I tried to look about me, beyond the forms of the women surrounding me. I glimpsed buildings, but none were familiar to me. Another snatch of panic fluttered in my stomach. I was lost. I had no idea where we were heading and no idea how to return to the hotel. Be calm, I again silently urged myself, London is full of cabs. But would any of them take a suffragette home?

Along the road we were marching I became aware of spectators. From the start people had stopped their business to gawp at us.[1] But now the spectators were no longer merely watching. Even over the noise of the

---

[1] What my mother would have made of me making such a spectacle of myself I shuddered to think. I could only have made things worse if I had marched in my petticoats.

song, I became aware of male voices. The words were difficult to distinguish, but the tone was hostile. We passed one man and I saw his face contorted in anger. Windows were opening. Men were hanging out of them, shaking their fists at us. We must be coming into the heart of the city, for there were more and more of them. Then the missiles began. Not from our side as I had feared, but people, both men and women began to throw things down from the windows. The contents of a bucket were launched over some women in front of me, who shrieked with alarm and revulsion. They were not to be the only victims.

And now I saw police lining the road. Perhaps they had been following us for some time, or perhaps they, unlike I, had always known where this march was headed. Surely I thought they would intervene. Insults were one thing, and I suspected the suffragettes were all too accustomed to them, but missiles? Stones, old books, even a saucepan landed close enough to me that I had to step quickly to avoid being hit. My anger took a different turn. We were unarmed women. We were being attacked! There were more and more police lining the road, but not one man moved to aid us.

As we turned a corner, marching into a square, where there was a platform waiting, no doubt intended for us to listen to speeches, where it was easy to block the exits — it was then they sent the horses in.

In the initial moments of the onslaught by the police the women held firm, but police both on foot and on horse waded into the ranks of women, batons raised. It quickly became clear it was not enough for them to disperse this march; they were intent on taking prisoners. And worse yet, they had no hesitation in using violence against us.

My first thought was to find Richenda. I twirled wildly on the spot, trying to see through the heaving masses and keep my balance. Surely, with her flame-red hair I would be able to spot her.

Near the centre of the square, bodies jostled me from all sides. The smell of perfume mingled unpleasantly with the smell of sweat. We had been marching hard and we were being forced closer and closer together. For now, I was caught among the women away from the police, who were skirting the edge of the square. Through the crowd I thought I caught sight of police vans blocking one of the square's exits. The shy girl who had stood on my left cringed fearfully, unable to move. "You need to get away from here," I told her. She was mere inches from me, but I had to yell so she could hear me. Instead of heeding me she curled in on herself, crouching lower to the ground. I hauled her up by the arm. "Keep moving," I shouted, "stay on your feet or the crowd will crush you!" She looked at me with wild and frightened eyes. I knew I could not leave her.

I pulled her after me, not making for an exit, but wading deeper into the crowd. "Richenda!" I called, but my voice was lost. The mood in the square was changing fast. The singing continued in snatches across the square, in groups and the single women who held firm, but mostly the air was shrill with cries of outrage and screams.

Some of the women had been carrying flags on poles. I saw these now raised as weapons. Who struck first I could not in all honesty say. It was mayhem. A woman pushed past me wielding her flag before her. She headed towards the side where we could now hear the whinnying of horses.

Hans will never forgive me if I do not find Richenda, I thought, but the likelihood of doing so seemed remote. Indeed, if I, and the terrified girl who had attached herself to me, were to get away, we had to go now.

I cursed Richenda a thousand times as I turned my back on her. I could only hope her stout form and strong temperament would bring her through. Even then I could not bring myself to believe that the London police would use force against women. I told myself they were only trying to frighten us.

I pushed through the crowd. The tidy rank and file had disintegrated. It seemed to me that the women were a mixture of those who were ripe for battle and those who desperately wanted to flee.

This is not a happy mix for any army in close quarters, for army we were about to become. The policemen advanced into the throng. Batons raised, they lashed out around them. I glimpsed one women, her straw hat askew and blood running down her face. Her companion, a matron long past middle years, thumped the policeman heartily with her flag, beating him off her colleague. Two men came up behind her and grasping her by the arms dragged her back, with no thought given to her age or fragility. I saw her mouth open, whether she was screaming or cursing I could not tell, but they bore her off. Her companion bloodied and confused stumbled back into the fray and I did not see her again.

To my right I heard the whinny of a horse. Unbelievably the police had ridden their horses into the heart of the crowd. Women scattered from the beasts' paths as the riders lashed out right and left with their batons. I tried to pull my charge out of the way, but I was too slow. The baton came down and caught her a glancing blow on the cheek. She gave a small cry and slumped to the ground, the horse above her. Without thinking I leapt for the horse's reins, and pulled it sharply round to the right, so the hooves fell close, but not on her. The rider struck at me with his baton, and with a strength I did not know I had I grabbed at his belt and hauled him from his seat.

The horse, wanting even less than its rider to be among the crowds, made off. The rider attempted to struggle to his feet, but already my actions had been noted. A cry of triumph arose around and women surged forward beating at the man with umbrellas, flags, reticules, and even in one old woman's case, her shoe. I might have feared for his life were it not that the unseating of the rider had been noticed and forces quickly despatched in our direction.

Within moments my arms were pulled behind me by two policemen who addressed me in such language that I had never heard before in my life. Instinct warned me this was no time to fight. These men's blood was up, but so was mine. I managed to twist hard to my right and bite one man savagely on the hand. I tasted blood.

The next moment a blow of such force landed on my head that the world went completely dark.

CHAPTER
SIX

Infamy! Infamy!

I woke slowly and in great pain. I was lying on something hard. As a child I had learned, from a particularly poisonous little girl who attended my father's Sunday School, not to open my eyes the moment I woke. Surprisingly it is a knack I have found useful in many situations. Having no idea where I was, but assuming I had been attacked and possibly kidnapped, I attempted to push aside the throbbing pain in my head and focus my attention on listening.

I have been concussed before and that fact I knew I was again allowed me to hope that my senses were not too addled. Still, it took a while for me to distinguish the sounds around me. Chiefly, I was aware of the scents of perspiration, dirt or dust — a strange grimy smell — and lastly the smell of a variety of perfumes, all conflicting horribly. Voices murmured around me. The words were indistinct, but they sounded to be all female. The inside of my head beat its nasty rhythm as I tried to understand how I came to be with many females. How were we all shut up together. Although my immediate memory was proving unhelpful, my mind provided me with an unpleasant flashback to the time I had almost become the inmate of an asylum.[1] I felt my body begin to tremble at the thought, but then I realised there was no sharp smell of cleaning fluid or other medicinal smell. So, I could not be there. There was also no smell of pigs, I thought. And then the memory of being shut in a pigsty awaiting execution with Fitzroy flooded back — but we had got out of that . . .

"Oh for heaven's sake, Euphemia, Wake Up!" cried the all too piercing voice of Richenda Stapleford. I opened my eyes. In front of me I saw bars, such as one might find in a police cell. I was lying on a dirty, wooden floor. Out of the corner of my eye I caught sight of a row of women's skirts. I pushed myself up using one hand, pausing half way as nausea almost overcame me.

Richenda Stapleford's face loomed over me. "Gosh, you look like a dead fish," she opined. "Try not to be sick. I doubt anyone would come and clear it up." I waited for a moment, catching my breath. "Where are we?"

"In jail," responded Richenda with a grim smile. She raised her voice. "It seems the King's police force now consider it their duty to attack and detain defenceless women." She put her arm under my mine and helped me up. I staggered against her, but Richenda's fondness for cake has made her sturdy. She helped me across to a wooden bench where two other women at once made way for me to sit.

---

[1] See my journal *A Death in the Asylum*.

As she said it my memory flooded back. "Richenda," I exclaimed, "how could you have tricked me into coming on a suffragette march? Hans will be furious."

Richenda's face set in a more than usually mulish expression. "Let him be! This was a peaceful protest. Do you realise since we have been put in here none of us have received medical attention. We have been given neither food nor water. We have been treated like animals."

"Did they take your names?" I asked.

"Yes, though some people gave obviously false ones."

"Did you?"

"Of course not. I want out of here as soon as possible. Marching and listening to speeches is one thing, but being attacked and thrown into jail is quite another. I can't even repeat the words the guard said to me when I asked him for a small slice of cake. You would have thought I was asking to be crowned queen. I memorised the number on his uniform. I shall tell Hans how badly I have been treated."

I reached up and gently touched the back of my head. "By being refused cake?"

Richenda had the grace to blush slightly. "Yes, I know you were injured . . . but honestly, Euphemia, you must have been fighting!"

I looked around. There were around twenty women crowded into a cell clearly meant for less. Their ages varied from an old crone, who was sitting on the floor picking at the edge of her skirt, to a young maid, who could have been no more than fourteen, who sat on the edge of the wooden bench, her face tear streaked, but her expression wooden. All the women were dishevelled and some had marks of blood on their clothes or their person.

"Don't worry. As soon as Hans hears about this he'll have us out of this terrible place," said Richenda more kindly. "He's an important man in the City. That will count for a lot."

"Yeah, and I'm royalty," said the crone, "Cockney royalty. And if I'm not mistaken, that one over there," she pointed to a woman with long blonde hair that flowed unhindered over her shoulders, sitting with her hands neatly in her lap as if she was awaiting a train, "is a ladyship. Ain't going to do any good. Coppers want to haul us all into court. Make an example of us. Show that we're wild hysterical women!" She laughed loudly, showing cracked and broken teeth. "I'm not saying that in my day I didn't get involved in a scrape or two, but this time! This time I was sitting quiet as you like on the edge of the square selling me flowers as usual and this copper drags me away from my pitch. Oi! I tells him. That's my livelihood you're leaving on the street. Then one of his mates kicked my buckets over with his big plates of meat. That was it. That was when I belted the one holding me with my stick." She sighed, and looked suddenly deflated, like a pile of rags on the floor. "Took me stick away, they did. Probably broke it or burnt it. Bastards. Can't get up without it." A spark of malice flickered in her eyes, "Reckon some of you fine folks are finally going to find out what it's like to be poor. To be treated like dirt. They ain't going to let any of you off. None of you at all. You mark my words. Stupid wenches trying to prove you're the equal of your men folk. Didn't you work out years ago that any one woman's worth three blokes — five? None of you have got the sense God gave you."

The cell had hushed to listen to this extra-ordinary outburst.

Someone began to applaud. It was the young woman who had been sitting so neatly. "There is much truth in what you say, madam," she said in a soft, well-spoken voice. "What we lack is an influence in the laws that govern the country. In law we are regarded as no more than chattels and that is an offence against every woman who has ever lived or shall ever be born. That is why we must protest. That is why we must win."

"If yer don't know how to influence your man by now, luv, I doubt there is any hope for you," said the old woman crudely, but without malice.

At this conversation that had been naturally stilled by the frightening nature of our surrounding broke loose once more. Debate raged and the atmosphere in the room lifted. Beyond the bars lay a long corridor that faced only a brick wall that had perhaps once been white washed. Richenda saw where I was looking. "I pressed my face against the bars. There is nothing to see."

"But what if we wish to use — the facilities," I blushed.

Richenda nodded at a bucket in the comer. "They are treating us like animals."

"Good God!" I said, shocked. "That must be some cruel joke. There is no privacy. Not simply from each other, but from any policeman who might choose to walk along that corridor. As if summoned by my prediction a police guard appeared at one edge of the bar. He wore a sergeant's stripes on his sleeve. His face was worn, and the veins in his nose clearly widened and split by drink. He regarded us with the same loathing a child might a particularly ugly specimen in the zoological gardens. Then he rang his baton along the bars. "Shut up, you whores!" he shouted.

As one the women quietened. And then almost at once they began to shout out and decry his foul accusation. Two more policemen appeared. They also ran their batons along the bars. The noise echoed in the close confines of the prison and was as intimidating as it was intended to be. Then on policeman pointed his baton at the young maid I had noticed earlier. "She'll do."

A fourth man appeared with keys at his belt. The three men entered, pushing back the other women with batons raised and dragged the screaming girl out.

"You cannot do this!" I screamed. "This is the King's England."

The guard who had called us such foul names pointed at me. "You, Euphemia St John, you're next!"

All faces turned to me. He knew my name. Of the thousands of women on that march they knew my name!

CHAPTER
SEVEN

Tension in the ranks and a most unexpected arrival

"That is outrageous!" exclaimed Richenda.

"It is not that unexpected," said the quiet woman, who had been sitting on the bench. She held out her hand to us. "Mary Hill. I have taken part in a number of marches and the behaviour you have just witnessed has become increasingly common, I am sad to say." She blushed slightly, "Please excuse my appearance. I lost my hat and all my pins in the commotion."

"What will they do with her?" I asked, thinking this was no time for sartorial concerns.

"They will ask her questions and attempt to determine if they should send her to the court for prosecution, hold her for longer or let her go. She is young, scared, and obviously working-class with no one to defend her. She is a natural target."

"For?" I pressed.

Mary sighed. "As you may be aware, some of our Sisterhood have reached the point of frustration at which they feel they must use violence to make their point. The police are keen to find these particular women and their associates."

"What has that got to do with that little girl?" demanded Richenda, her maternal instincts seemingly aroused.

"They think she will be easy to intimidate," I answered for Mary. "That is correct, is it not? They hope she may be the weakest link in a chain."

"Exactly," said Mary. "I am not among those favouring violence, but if I were I would choose my tools with care. Ones able to withstand questioning and, if necessary, to endure force-feeding."

"Force-feeding?" echoed Richenda blankly. The concept clearly baffled her.

"Some of us believe in passive resistance, and if imprisoned, we will go on hunger strike. Obviously, the Establishment does not care to see any of us die or be released so malnourished. They fear it would create public sympathy. They have devised a manner to force food into those who abstain."

"Doesn't sound too bad," said Richenda, who had never knowingly turned away food.

"Imagine being held down, a tube forced down your mouth, on down through your chest and into your stomach. A funnel is attached to the end and liquid food is poured into you without your consent. If you struggle, damage done to your body may be considerable. As well as humiliation you may risk permanent disability."

I sat down upon the floor. The pain in my head had not ceased and I now felt decidedly queasy. "I cannot believe that this is happening to free women in this century."

"There is nothing free about our position, my dear," said Mary kindly. She crouched down next to me. "When the guard returns I shall see if they will allow a doctor to visit you. You have gone alarmingly pale. Were you harmed in the fracas?"

"I was hit on the head with a baton by a policeman on a horse," I said surprisingly myself with my succinctness.

"Pulled him right off his seat, she did," remarked another woman coming over to join us. She wore the plain dress of a servant off duty. Her face was freckled and her hair scraped back into a bun. I judged her to be in her mid to late twenties. "Saw it myself or I'd never have believed it. Hauled him off by his belt and onto the ground."

"He was over-balanced, attempting to reach a young girl who was with me." Recalling the incident more clearly, I looked around the cell, but the girl I had attempted to rescue was not with us."

"Well, good for you," said our new friend. "A bit of sauce for the gander!" She thrust out her hand to me "Abigail Stokes. Pleasure to meet a sister in arms."

"Euphemia St John. He was about to trample a girl underfoot. I had little other recourse."

Abigail frowned, large creases appeared along her forehead and she looked extremely formidable. "Hmm," she more or less snorted. "They deserved no less."

"I cannot agree that violence will advance our cause," said Mary in her well-modulated voice.

Abigail sneered and retreated. "I don't think we meet with her approval," said Richenda in her usual loud and carrying tone. "So much for sisterhood!"

I grimaced inwardly. My memory had returned to me enough that I recalled a remarkable number of women from all ranks had been more than happy to indulge in violence. "Richenda, I really think you should keep your voice down," I said quietly. "We must all co-exist in this extremely inadequate cell until our captors are prepared to release us."

"I'm not staying here!" announced Richenda. She rose and approached the bars. "Guard!" she cried loudly. "Guard, I say! I demand to be released. I am Lady Richenda, Mrs Hans Muller. I must be released at once."

"Is she really a lady?" asked Mary quietly of me.

"Her brother is a Baronet, their father the first ennobled. I rather fear the family has been playing fast and loose with titles ever since."

Mary nodded. "That would only make her an Honourable. And she has married a commoner too."

"She has a heart of gold," I said defensively. Richenda continued to yell.

Mary gave a small smile. "That may be so, but if she does not quiet she will cause trouble both within and without this cell."

But before any further altercation could occur a guard did appear at the bars. "Shut your trap," he told Richenda bluntly. Richenda at once began to protest even more loudly. The man resorted to running his baton along the bars mere inches from her face. The noise as well as the threat caused her to back away.

"Right, Euphemia St John, you're up next. I can fetch men to drag you or you can come quiet like."

Richenda clutched my sleeve. "Don't leave me," she begged.

"They are offering to allow me to walk to the interview. I take this as a good sign," I murmured to her. "I will come," I said to the guard.

"Right, you others, back off. One blow of my whistle and twenty men will answer." What these men would do when they arrived was emphasised by another beating of the bars. I rose unsteadily and made my way to door. The guard opened the cell, his whistle at his lips. I passed through and he relocked the door. He poked me in the back with his truncheon. "That way!"

He was a small man and an ugly one, much like his temperament. I resisted the temptation to turn, wrest the baton from his grasp, and beat him over his head with it. I felt far too dizzy to try such a manoeuvre. I did however turn and give him a look learnt from my mother — a woman of four foot eleven inches, who swore that she had once reduced a Duke to tears. "I will go with you," I said coldly, "there is no need to poke me." I thought I saw a flicker of surprise or perhaps even concern in his eyes, but he covered it quickly and gestured onwards with his baton.

I was taken along several narrow brick passageways. I noted windows, small, barred, and up against the ceiling. Light came from them in dusty, dull shafts. Could we be below ground? I grew increasingly uncomfortable. We passed no other cell or office. I was alone with this man. Just as I was seriously considering knocking him to the ground and attempting to flee, we reached a wooden door. The guard knocked on it with his truncheon. A muffled voice answered. The guard opened the door and pushed me forward.

Light blinded me. After the dimness of the corridors it took my eyes time to adjust, but I recognised the voice at once.

"Goodness, Euphemia! What have you done to yourself!"

"Fitzroy!" I exclaimed and slumped to the ground in a dead faint.

CHAPTER
EIGHT

A most unusual supper in familiar and not totally unpleasant company

"Good God, man! Fetch a doctor. She is badly injured. I will hold you personally accountable if she has suffered any lasting harm."

My eyes flickered open. "You sound cross," I said.

Fitzroy's grey eyes bored down into mine. "I am exceedingly cross." He had been leaning over me, but after this comment raised his face. "And when I am exceedingly cross I become exceedingly dangerous." I heard the sound of feet running away. A smile flickered across my face and I slipped from consciousness once more.

"Ow!"

Fitzroy slapped me again. "I am sorry, Euphemia, but if you are badly concussed then it is imperative you stay awake."

"I understand," I said, pushing myself up to a sitting position. Fitzroy helped me over to a chair. "Frankly, Euphemia, I am extremely annoyed with you."

"You do not believe in the suffragette cause?" Fitzroy dragged a chair round from the other side of the desk that lay between us and sat next to me. He swatted away my idea as another man might a fly. "I have told you previously on more than one occasion I believe your sex is under-rated, but protests while Asquith is in power are pointless."

I put up my hand to rub my sore cheek. "Why?"

Fitzroy gave a bark of laughter. "Because the man only values women one way. On their backs!"

My eyes felt like they were popping from their sockets. I must indeed have pulled an unusual expression, because Fitzroy laughed again. "In some ways you are such an innocent. Euphemia, some men will only ever see a woman, at best, as a breeding vessel, and at worst as a plaything. Despite all the suffragettes' protests he simply does not feel they are important enough to take notice of their pleas."

"But that's terrible," I exclaimed.

"In any fight it is important to understand your opponent," Fitzroy said seriously. "I fear that in this situation both sides are underestimating each other to a dangerous degree."

I felt myself become a little dizzy. Fitzroy put out an arm to steady. "Where is that damn doctor? You're no use to me like this!"

Despite all I had been through this brought a real smile to my lips. "So we get to the heart of the matter."

"Later," commanded Fitzroy. "After you have seen the doctor and eaten a decent meal."

My head began to feel a little clearer and for the first time I took in his appearance properly. Fitzroy is a spy in the service of the crown. In general he concerns himself solely in the matter of international politics, but our paths have crossed more than once. Normally a most conservative dresser, he was wearing an extremely well cut and obviously expensive suit. His face had acquired more lines, but then when I had last encountered him he had recently been tortured for some days. I was relieved to see that his arm had mended, and while it did not escape me that from time to time he flexed his fingers tentatively, it appeared that all the obvious injuries he had incurred were healed. His face, pleasant enough to look at but one unremarkable in a crowd, was paler than usual, and his cheeks thinner and more gaunt that before. "You look much better than when I last saw you," I remarked, "but not quite your normal self."

Seeing I now seemed able to keep to my seat unaided Fitzroy began pacing the room like the proverbial caged tiger. "Even I must admit I am not yet back to my top form," he growled. "That's why I am here dealing with this mess." He opened his mouth to say more, but a small balding man clutching a doctor's bag burst into the room. He moped his face with an enormous handkerchief he pulled from his pocket. Sweat beaded all across his face. He was on the stout side and I realised must have been going at quite a pace. "So sorry," he puffed. "Came as quick as I could. Where's the patient?"

"If you need me to tell you that," snapped Fitzroy, "I doubt you are the man to help us."

"The suffragette!" exclaimed the doctor in accents of strong disapproval.

52

"This lady here," said Fitzroy, his voice so stern and crisp it sliced through the atmosphere like a knife.

"I really don't know . . . " muttered the doctor, setting his bag down on the table. "All these women are hysterics. What seems to be the particular trouble with you, my dear?"

"She is not your dear," growled Fitzroy, "She is one of us. And if you will take the trouble of opening your eyes you will see she has suffered a severe blow to the head."

The doctor's manner changed immediately. "You sent a lady into that scrum!" he said. "I cannot support such action."

"Send a memo," sneered Fitzroy. "Now see to the lady."

A little while later my head was bandaged, I had been made to swallow something most unpleasant, and told to avoid further exertion for the foreseeable future. Fitzroy, through much shouting, threats, and by essentially terrifying the guard and any other personnel who were foolish enough to come near us, had managed to procure me a chaise longue to lie upon, while the desk was converted into a dining table set and laid for two.

When the last poor underling had left the room, Fitzroy shut the door and locked it, dropping the key in his pocket. I regarded him from my prone position. "Should that worry me?" I asked.

"I do not care for us to be interrupted. Now come to the table and dine, Euphemia. It will make you feel much better than you realise." He poured me a glass of red wine. "Only one," he said. "It will strengthen you."

The dinner set before us consisted of grilled steak, roasted potatoes, petits pois, carrots and a thick dark gravy. A smaller table set to one side help a selection of puddings and custards. A cushion had been placed on my chair and a leaned back against it gratefully. "Hardly the forced feeding I had been led to expect," I said dryly.

Fitzroy sliced through his steak, which bled onto his plate. He saw my expression. "Don't be concerned, yours was cooked for longer than mine. I am aware that even the most strong-hearted of women do not tend to like bloody meat."

"My companions?" I asked.

Fitzroy sighed. "The majority of them have been questioned — gently — and released. The ones most directly involved in the violence or who have questionable records have been detained."

"Richenda?"

"I am trying to eat! I have had nothing since lunchtime!"

"A terrible state of affairs, I agree — but Richenda?"

"Released. Though it took some doing. From what I hear she waded into the fray laying about her like a woman possessed."

I nodded. "She does have a temper."

"Even her darling husband couldn't have got her out if I hadn't . . . " he let the sentence trail off.

"Is that meant to suggest that I owe you a favour? Because if it is," I added sternly, once more bringing my mother to mind, "I think after the incident at the pig farm you remain firmly in my debt."

Fitzroy grinned and raised his glass to me. "I do indeed, but what I am going to ask you to do is not for me, but as a representative of the Crown."

I groaned. "You mean for King and Country? Not again!"

CHAPTER
NINE

Fitzroy bemoans his lack
of entertainment

"The thing is," said Fitzroy as he spooned a strawberry blancmange onto my dessert plate, "that the suffragettes have started getting involved in violence and they are doing rather well. From the current informants I have managed to gather that they . . . "

"You have them informing on one another?" I exploded. "So much for sisterhood indeed."

"The violence has been extreme, Euphemia. We are not talking about the smashing of a few windows any longer. Telephone exchanges have been destroyed. Railway carriages badly damaged. This is occurring at a time when the international situation is far from stable and I do not need to tell you how important communication and other infrastructures during are during what may soon become the darkest of times."

I shivered at his words. "You believe that —" I began, but he interrupted me.

"I am not here to speak with you of international affairs. Finish your dessert. I will tell what has brought me into the situation over coffee."

"They're going to bring us coffee?" I asked astonished. "We are hardly dining at the Ritz."[1]

"They will if they know what is good for them," snarled Fitzroy and fell on his own portion of spotted dick as if it had somehow offended him.

When plates had been removed, coffee poured and we were alone once more, Fitzroy grew serious. "I do most definitely need your help, but if you are not well enough to continue I must ask you to say so before I disclose further information."

"Will I be required to do anything energetic?" I asked for my head still throbbed.

"You will be placed back among the detained women. At times you will be removed for questioning — or so the others will think. In actuality you will be dining with me and discussing what you may have uncovered."

"So I am to be spy?" I said bridling.

"An embryonic one," said Fitzroy. "You barely have any training, but I do not think you will be in any danger." He dabbed at his mouth with his napkin. "Remind me, when you are feeling more yourself, to show you some basic self-defence moves. By all reports you were taken most easily. Though I give you full marks for pulling the man out of his saddle. I take it he was completely unbalanced at the time?"

"That is largely accurate," I admitted. "But I'm not sure I am comfortable being . . . " I met his clear, cold, grey gaze. I swallowed. "I mean . . . " His gaze

---

[1] Though in all fairness the food was superb.

challenged me to decry his lifelong profession. I gave way and said somewhat piteously, "Why?"

"Because someone has died, Euphemia, and I am almost certain that one of the women in the cell with you will know who caused his death. More than that, though, I need to know if his death was intended."

"How did he die?"

"A fire bomb was placed in a railway carriage. When the blaze was extinguished two bodies were recovered, one of a young suffragette and the other of a man of, shall we say, significance."

"And it happened at the same time as the march? You think the protest was a deliberate diversion?"

Fitzroy leaned back in his chair. "I do so enjoy conversing with you," he remarked.

"Who died?"

"The young woman's name was Aggie Phelps, a known suffragette of the more militant persuasion. Twenty-nine years old, spinster, working as one of those shop girls, who are given lodging in the store. Her colleagues describe her as intelligent, but of a somewhat sour disposition. She had a strong dislike of male authority and was currently on her last warning."

I noticed Fitzroy did not refer to any notes. No, notes could be incriminating, I told myself, and I did my best to retain the information. Whatever the doctor had given me had eased the throbbing, but I still felt as if there was an iron band around my temples that was intent on squeezing my poor brain.

"The man," continued Fitzroy, either not noticing or not caring to notice my discomfort, "was Sir Aubrey

Wilks, a senior civil servant. Unmarried, or perhaps 'married to his job' is a better description. He had been known to frequent the higher class of brothel for his amusement, but not to avail himself of disporting with his own sex. He has no connection with the suffragette movement that I can discover. Though, of course, I have only been looking since this morning. He was not someone on Edward's watchlist."

I swallowed hard, trying desperately not to think of how my mother would react to this conversation. Fitzroy has never amended his manner around me to suggest he thinks of me as a member of a weaker sex or a being with fragile sensibilities.[1] The mention of Edward, the man with bushy eyebrows, a discreet office, and a network of informants across Great Britain, also sent a shiver down my spine. He is less amiable than Fitzroy.

"The girl Aggie was not known to be a . . . " I left the sentence hanging. I might be quite capable of following Fitzroy's train of thought,[2] but there was no reason why I could not speak as a lady.

"She was not of the appearance or breeding necessary to procure her a position among the establishments Sir Aubrey preferred." He shrugged.

---

[1] I have seen him do so with other women at superior social gatherings, so I know he is capable of treating a lady as a lady, but he never does so with me. I am unsure, but I believe from him that this may be a compliment.

[2] Being brought up alongside farmyard animals has proved most helpful in this

"And even if on some whim he had had occasion to lower his standards, I can discover no scrap of evidence that she was ever a street-walker."

"But you think she might have planted or somehow set of this firebomb?"

Fitzroy inclined his head to one side, "My information suggests she may have been connected to a cell responsible for the destruction of a telephone exchange last month. She has certainly been arrested for window-smashing, and was only spared jail because a foolish man in a wig judged her to be of a respectable position and a woman of promise, who had been led astray by more devious women."

"You do not believe that so?"

"I think she was quick and clever, dedicated to her cause and if she was caught in a fire bombing of her own making it was by accident and not design. I also happen to think that from smashing windows to firebombing is a big step, but to be frank my interest in this matter is Wilks. He was a man of some standing in the Civil Service, and more to the point some of his old school fellows are of even more standing, and want to know what happened to their old chum."

"Could Aggie's death be a suicide and Wilks's death a collateral effect?" I countered.

Fitzroy took a deep breath. "So far something of that nature has not yet occurred. It would indeed be a powerful statement." He took another sip of his coffee. "You know, Euphemia, I am very glad you are on our side. You would make a formidable opponent."

"How do you know I do not support votes for women?" I returned hotly.

"I suspect you do," replied Fitzroy, "but you would never condone violence, especially where innocent life is endangered. And your upbringing would preclude you from supporting self-destruction altogether." His face softened. "I do believe women will one day get the vote and that they deserve it, too, but now is not the time for that particular battle. We will face such peril on these isles that we will all be forced to stand together."

"You are suggesting that war will soon come to our shores."

Fitzroy's eyes raised in surprise. "I very much hope such an occurrence will not come to *our* shores. It will however not be long before the Balkans erupt into war and that will be the start of it all." He sighed heavily. "And here I am looking into the death of a civil servant."

"A far less exciting experience than being on the ground at the beginning of a war," I remarked.

Fitzroy's eyes sparkled. "Exactly. Where is the adventure in this?"

"I shall choose not to be insulted by that remark, but simply remind you that justice is a higher calling and one that you should not be shamed to embrace."

"This," he gestured to the room around us, "is not living. This is the slow death march of time within the boundaries of petty politics that will never shape a better world. One day, Euphemia, I shall have to take you somewhere exciting."

I shivered at the thought.

"In the meantime," continued Fitzroy, "could you be a good girl and discover what, if anything, the women in cell know about Wilks's death. In return I shall ensure that no mention of your part in the fracas is ever mentioned." He rose and gave me a quick smile that did not quite reach his eyes. "Besides, I am sure you would be happy enough to do this without reward, seeing as you have such a high regard for justice."

"How am I . . .?" but Fitzroy was already unlocking the door and calling for the guard to return me to me cell. My hands were manacled behind my back. I gave Fitzroy a furious look. "For verisimilitude," he said. "Not too rough," he added to the guard as the man began to hustle me from the room.

"Euphemia," Fitzroy said as I was exiting the door, "if you do feel ill again, have one of your compatriots summon the guard. I will ensure there is medical aid on offer for you."

"A hairbrush would be more useful," I countered, but he merely smiled his cold smile again and closed the door in my face.

"Sorry about this," said the guard as he took my upper arm in a vice-like grip, "but if they others don't believe it they may turn nasty on you."

"Ouch, does it have to be quite that sore?"

"Believe me a few bruises to show the others will quieten any suspicions of where you have been. Though you'll need to try not to get too close to anyone for a while. There's wine on your breath. Sometimes Fitzroy is too flash for his own good."

"You're one of his men?"

"Hush," said the guard. "We're getting near the cells. No, I work for Mr Edward. You can call me Mark. Fitzroy's on secondment due to his recent injuries, but I heard you knew about all that."

"Hmm," I nodded. When matters of state are involved I have learnt to keep my mouth shut. As if he had read my thoughts, the guard looked at me approvingly. "I'm the only one in here. If another guard is taking you out it's probably not somewhere you want to be going."

I swallowed hard. Weak as I was, I imagined I would find it hard to resist a man bent on dragging me out of the cell, though the heavens knew I would do my damnedest. "And I really am sorry about this," said Mark as we turned the corner and came up against the bars of a large cell. He kept his grip on my arm as he unlocked the cell. Then he pushed me in with such force that I landed on my hands and knees. He spat at me — though I am glad to say his spittle did not actually reach my person. "Stupid whore," he said and clanged the door shut. He locked the door and ran his baton loudly along the bars as he walked away. The noise made my tender head ring.

I sat back on heels and surveyed my surroundings. Eight women looked down at me. None of them were smiling.

CHAPTER
TEN

Thrown to the lions
(or rather, lionesses)

Richenda was not in the cell. Our number had been reduced to nine. My task was now to interrogate these eight women discreetly. I did not have pen and paper to hand for obvious reason, but even if I had I would have been loath to record anything another might read. My thoughts about whether it might be safe to write in Latin served only to remind me that I had forgotten many of my conjugations through lack of use. Instead, as I made tentative moves towards knowing my cellmates, our proximity making this a necessity and thus not too lacking in subtlety, I attempted to make mental notes in the manner I imagined Fitzroy might. Of course he was used to this and I was not. For the first time I actively missed having either Bertram, or even a sulky Rory, with me on my adventures. I felt very alone.

And so it seemed did little Maisie Dawson, the maid who had been taken away before me. She was the first to come over and ask in the quietest of voices, "Are you alright, m'um?"

"I am, thank you." I smiled at her and brushed back a few stray locks. "A bit roughly used, but I will survive. I'm Euphemia," I added, holding out my hand.

The girl brushed away a tear and tentatively took my hand. "Maisie Dawson." She gulped. "I think you're right brave, miss. They were horrible to me."

"Did they beat you?" asked the freckled face woman who had been so forthright before.

"N-no," stammered Maisie. "Are they likely to?"

"Depends on whether or not we go on hunger strike! Which of course we will if they threaten to hold us here much longer!"

"Perhaps it will all be sorted out much sooner than you expect," I suggested, noticing Maisie's terrified expression.

"My name is Abigail Stokes and I am proud to be a long-standing member and activist for women's rights! Onward, sisters!"

I blinked at this forthrightness. "We may have to suffer to reach our aim, but it will be worth it," continued this redoubtable matron.

The woman, who had been sitting calmly and was particularly well-spoken, came across to the little group. "Maisie, I am Mary Hill," she said kindly, "and I assure you that you need do nothing that you do not wish to do. We may all be united in our belief women should have a say in the running of their own country, but we are not," and she gave Abigail a stern look at this point, "all of the persuasion that hunger strikes or even the indulgence in violence is the way forward. If you are polite and co-operative with the police force I am sure we will all be quickly released."

Maisie gave Mary and I muttered "thanks, m'ums" and disappeared over to the corner.

"Quiet as a mouse," opined Abigail not bothering to keep the scorn from her voice.

"Young and frightened," retorted Mary Hill. "That she came on the march at all shows great courage."

Abigail gave a loud sniff. "What would the likes of you know about courage? Bet you're sitting pretty. I bet your nob of a hubby will have you out of here in a jiffy."

"I am unmarried," said Mary calmly and quietly, "and if the imprisonment of Mrs Pankhurst and others has shown us nothing else, it has proved that rank is no protection against imprisonment."

"Well, they will have to put us up before the magistrate soon," said Abigail. Then she turned on me, "Unless there's something *you* know that I don't!"

To my horror I felt the blood rushing into my face. Why had Fitzroy asked me to spy on these women? It was a task I was most unsuited to.

Mary came to my rescue. "Oh, hush," she said, "for a women who protests to support the Sisterhood you appear to be doing your best to set us each against the other."

Abigail fairly glowered at this, but turned her back on us to go over and talk to two older women, who were dressed very much alike, sitting close together and regarding us all with great suspicion.

"They," said Mary Hill to me, "are Eunice and Jasmine Pettigrew. Both of them retired teachers and on a much reduced income. I do not believe they are twins. Although they dress alike and appear to be of similar age." She smiled at me. "I have met them at previous meetings. They live near to me. They are resolute in their belief in the suffrage movement and also that the rest of the world is against them, poor things. I fear they have both had a very hard life and have learned to cling only to each other for support."

"You are most observant," I remarked.

"I have had a little longer than you to become acquainted with our companions. In situations when one is confined in such close quarters I find it helpful to assess who I am with. Sadly, while we might all be suffragettes, of late the cause has become much divided. It is not uncommon for fights to break out in the cells. At least, until the confinement takes a crueller turn."

"You have been arrested before."

"I do appear to have the unfortunate knack of being arrested," said Mary, her eyes twinkling, "however, I have never been detained formally in prison. It is not just words. I do not believe in anything more than passive protest. Anything else gives the establishment leave to demonise us and to use violence towards our persons."

"Does that really happen?" I asked.

"I am afraid so," said Mary, her voice very low. She cast a quick look towards Maisie, but the young woman had remarkably curled herself up and appeared to be fast asleep. "It is why I was glad of your help in dealing with Miss Stokes. Her actions could make life for us all very difficult."

"Do you know who the other women with us are?" I asked hopefully. Could it be that Mary had already done most of my job for me?

"Constance Woodley," she said pointing discreetly to a blonde-haired woman with a round face and slightly fuller figure. "We had an interesting conversation. She is the wife of a doctor and the mother of two young children. She is most conflicted concerning her role as a campaigner and a mother. She has one daughter and one son, and has remarked to me many times that already she sees such unfairly different futures for them both. Her husband assumes her son will also train as a doctor, but Constance feels her daughter is the brighter of the two."

"She wants her daughter to train in medicine?" I asked amazed.

"It is not so unusual for women to train in the higher education systems. I, myself, studied mathematics at Oxford. Though of course, despite sitting the exams, and passing them, I have not been awarded a degree."

"Why?"

"Because I am a woman, my dear, and women cannot be awarded degrees. I have met many intelligent women, from all walks of life. It is one of the main reasons that I joined the movement. It makes little sense to me that our country should not make use of the talents of its citizens regardless of their gender." Her eyes shone brightly. "By the very nature of our different genders men and women must perceive things differently. Imagine what a disciplined and well-trained female mind might do with some of the great problems of our age if they were allowed to bring their intelligence to bear!"

"Indeed," I said. "When you put it like that the argument is unassailable."

Mary laughed heartily at that. "Sadly, I fear only another woman would agree with me."

"No," I said, "I can think of more than one man of my acquaintance who would agree with you."[1] I took the plunge and changed the subject. "Who are our other two companions?"

"The middle-aged lady I believe is an actual Lady. She has given her name as Martha Lake, but I suspect that was to spare her husband. The other woman, perhaps in her thirties, with the long black hair trailing down her back — I suspect she lost her hat in the fray — has given her name to the sergeant as Angela Blackwood. I have not yet had a chance to converse with her. She is terribly thin and frowns a great deal, which I believe has put the others off approaching her. She certainly alarms me. Anyway, perhaps you might like to tell me about yourself, Euphemia, now I have answered all the questions I can."

I felt myself blush again. "I am the daughter of a Vicar," I said truthfully. I felt I had enough duplicity

---

[1] Actually, I could only think of one: Fitzroy. Both Bertram and Rory still needed my continued input to convince them of the durability of my sex. Though under my tutelage, if it is not too immodest to say, I do feel they have come a very long way.

playing my role for Fitzroy without adding further lies. "My father believed women should be educated. He did not go as far as sending me away for education," I gave a little shrug, "Though in all honesty I doubt our finances would have stood the expense. However, he taught me to how think analytically, a very little mathematics, allowed me to read great literature, and introduced me to the classics, including some of the ancient languages." I blushed again, aware that I was attempting to prove to this woman I was as intelligent as she.

"Allowed you to read," said Mary and broke off sighing. "That any woman should have to be given permission to read!"

"I did not mean it like that," I protested hotly. "My father was a good man! The very best."

"Ahh, he has passed," said the all-too-acute Mary. "I'm sorry, Euphemia. I meant no offence. For a man of his generation to educate you so he must have been exceptional."

"I am now companion to Richenda Muller," I said quickly, before my background could be further explored. "Her husband is in banking and the owner of a neat little country estate that is a marvel of prosperity and efficiency."

"And how does he feel about his wife's actions?"

"I don't believe he had any idea of the strength of her feelings. Even I had no idea that she was bringing us to this march. I thought we were coming on a shopping expedition!"

"But your clothes . . . " began Mary. Then she added, "Ah, she bought these for you."

"She said she wanted me to have a signature style. It never occurred to me that these colours were also those of the Sisterhood. You see, she has never had much in the way of style or colour co-ordination. I feel bad saying so but it is quite true —" I broke off. "I feel so foolish."

"It sounds to me as if your employer dressed you in the campaign colours because she either felt too afraid or too embarrassed to wear them herself."

I winced at this. "She is the most generous of employers. We have been through so much together."

Mary raised an eyebrow. I lifted my chin. "We were on the *Carpathia*. Such an experience changes and bonds people."

"Indeed, I imagine it could, but essentially I believe character is set when one is quite young and that people cannot change who they fundamentally are whatever their experiences in later life."

"What a very dark perspective!"

A shadow crossed Mary's face. "I fear unpalatable though these thoughts may be, they are the truth. I have found them borne out as truth time and time again in my life."

I sensed a story behind Mary's words, but before I could press her further, they was another ringing of the bars.

"That will be the guard bringing us our evening gruel," said Mary. "I do hope they have not spat in it, as they are wont to do!"

I looked at her aghast. I felt sincerely grateful towards Fitzroy for the first time since my incarceration. At least he had seen I was fed properly, but whether he would continue to do I had no idea.

Three guards, two bearing trays of bowls, opened the door enough to shove the trays through. Then another appeared and lobbed bread into the cell. Most of the crusts fell upon the filthy floor, but one hit Abigail Stokes above the eye. "Oi! That hurt!" she yelled. "It's bloody stale."

I tried hard not to smile.

CHAPTER
ELEVEN

Issues of trust and cake

The women sipped unhappily at the gruel, but wary of dark mentions of force-feeding, it seemed that no one wanted to leave a full bowl. The bread proved more of a challenge. Eunice Pettigrew opined sourly that "it was a surprise they should gift us with something more useful for digging an escape tunnel than eating." A small ripple of amusement ran through the room. Her sister Jasmine followed her quip by suggested it might be more useful as a weapon, but unlike her sister's strong if sour voice, Jasmine's was weak and whispery. No one paid her much attention with the exception of Abigail Stokes. A lump already blossomed above one eye where the crust had caught her. With anyone else I might have offered sympathy, but my head ached and I longed for sleep. I felt I could not bear any more of her sharp-tongued hostility. I smiled at little Maisie, who had awoken for the food, but remained curled tightly into her chosen corner.

I observed Mary sighing and crumbling her bread into the gruel. I tried to do the same, but found my fingers were not strong enough. A lassitude had fallen upon the cell. Abigail and perhaps Mary had expected us to held overnight, but in the rest of our small group I espied a weary astonishment. I suspected Eunice and Jasmine had thought their age would protect them. Constance Woodley frowned into her gruel and I thought I detected the glint of tears on her cheeks. I assumed she missed her children. I knew very little about motherhood. My mother had not been the doting kind. And Richenda's adopted daughter, Amy, remained a mixed bundle of joys and difficulties. I found myself wondering if Hans or Merry would be reading her a bedtime story tonight. An indulgence my mother would have decried as spoiling and ridiculous, but I had more than once read Amy her story and seen her fieriness fade under the weariness of the day as she slipped into sleep. I had discovered that a sleeping child could easily burrow into one's heart. How much worse must it be for Constance who had left her own little ones behind?

Martha Lake suddenly stood up and began to pace back and forth. In our overcrowded state this action disturbed us all. When she stood on my foot for the fourth time, I rose from my seat on the bench and inquired if I could be of assistance.

Martha lowered her face to mine. Close to, her skin contained more lines than I realised and I mentally readjusted my estimate of age upwards. "Do you know," she asked me in strangled, but refined accents, "how one summons the man to use the necessities?"

Unfortunately Abigail Stokes overheard us and gave a crack of coarse laughter. "That'll be the bucket in the corner, milady!"

74

Martha paled. "She cannot be serious?" she asked me.

At this point Constance came across to us. "I believe with the help of some other ladies we can arrange some privacy, but I fear that is indeed the basic commode we must use."

"Never," said Martha.

Constance gave her a gentle smile. "Sadly, it is not within our gift to control the tides of nature."

"Oh, dear God," said Martha. "This is unbearable."

Under Constance's guidance, we managed to surround the bucket, so that each woman could use it in a semblance of privacy. We were all more than aware that only bars separated us from the view of any passing guard.

Even Abigail was not exempt from the natural happenings of the human form and also had to take advantage of our makeshift water closet. I was extremely glad the bucket provided was on the larger side.

It was a humbling experience for us all. I imagined that if Rory or Bertram had been forced to endure such an experience they would have retreated to their individual areas and turned their backs, but with us women the hardship had bonded us. We exchanged friendly "good nights" and jocular hopes that we might sleep well, as we laid down in the darkness and prepared for rest.

To my surprise I did sleep well. I woke as dawn crept through the bars of the window. The light was weak, so I surmised the day was newly broken, I blinked to bring the cell into focus. I appeared to be the only one awake. Around me the women lay in various attitudes of reclining. Some had lain fully on the floor, like Abigail and Maisie. The Pettigrew sisters had slept sitting on the bench, leaning against the wall and each other. Their chins were sunk deep on their chests and as I watched Eunice uttered a snorting sound. Martha Lake had fallen onto one side and took up more than her fair share of the bench. Two other dark shapes on the floor I took to be Angela and Mary.

My headache had fled, but my back felt as stiff as a board. I wiggled my toes experimentally. They worked. I sat up carefully. Pain shot through my lower back and I almost cried out. I would not have been surprised if I had actually creaked as I pushed myself up to a sitting position.

"Euphemia St John," came a male voice behind me. "You're wanted."

Close to the bars was a man's face, illuminated in a most unflattering manner by the small lantern he held.

"For goodness' sake, be quiet!" I commanded. "You'll wake them." The man snorted and unlocked the door. "And send a man to change the bucket. It will be neede again when they awaken."

The man banged the door shut as I stepped through. He locked the door and then caught me in a painful armlock. Taken by surprise I could only gasp. "I don't know who you think you are," he spat in my ear, "but I don't take my orders from whores like you!" He did not allow me to walk myself, but frogmarched me down the corridor. I twisted my neck to look back at him. "For

76

heaven's sake," I began, and I intended to finish *you can drop the act now they can no longer see us*, when I saw the maniacal glint in his eye. This was not, as I had supposed, one of Fitzroy's men. Then I recalled Mark had said he was the one here. I felt a wave as fear. Where was I being taken and why, if not to the spy? Mary's and Abigail's warnings wormed their way into my treacherous heart, which began to beat most alarmingly fast.

"Frightened now, are you?" asked the hateful voice at my ear. "So you should be. This place is being soft on you women. At my last station we knew how to treat you. With chains. With whips. It's all your kind are good for. The good Lord gave you a place and you should keep it. Those that won't deserve all they get as far as I'm concerned. Women like you are fit for only one thing!"

At this end of this charming speech he thrust me through a door. "Ten minutes. That's your lot," he growled, and slammed the door behind me. The small room had no windows and was lit only by a candle lantern on the table. Sat on a small hard chair was the last person I had expected to see: Richenda Muller. In front of her was a box.

"Oh for heaven's sake, Euphemia," she cried, "what on earth have you got yourself into now?"

I collapsed into the chair. "Richenda, this was all your idea!"

Richenda pushed the box towards me. "Cake. It has been examined." I opened the lid to find an extravagant, rich, and frankly over-decorated monstrosity that even in the best of times would have made my stomach lurch. I recognised it as one of Richenda's favourites. It had been cut into sliver-thin slices, which I presumed was the examination. I recognised it for the peace offering it was.

"Thank you," I said, "but I would so much like to have known where we were going."

"You really did not guess? Even when I made you wear that dress. I thought you were meant to be unfashionably intelligent?"

I hung my head. "Perhaps I should have guessed."

"But what on earth made you get in with a terrorism cell?"

My head jerked up at that. "I am not and never have been involved with anyone who advocates violence!"

"The chief inspector I spoke to said you pulled a policeman off his horse."

"Have you been here all night?" I asked, astonished.

"It took me a while to convince them to let me see you. Hans called the station, but it did not have much effect. Bertram is on his way."

I blinked. "Why? What?"

"Well, obviously I cannot leave you here, and I cannot ask Hans to leave Amy. She needs one of us there and Bertram has helped you solve those little puzzles of yours before, so . . . ."

"What? How?"

"I don't believe for a moment that you would be involved in a firebombing, but both Hans and I have failed to convince the police, so the only option left is for Bertram and I to solve the case."

CHAPTER
TWELVE

Richenda plots and I despair

I could think of nothing worse than Richenda blundering around in what might prove to be a highly dangerous situation. Where on earth was Fitzroy when I needed him? I took a deep breath. "Richenda, Hans is a wonderful man, but Amy needs you."

Richenda sniffed valiantly. "So the quicker we get this over with the better. The early morning newspapers have named the man that died as Sir Aubrey Wilks. When I telephoned Hans he said he had never heard of him. I suppose I could ask Richard, but I don't trust him not to meddle to your disadvantage."

"Indeed," I said dryly. Richenda's brother was something of a nemesis to me.

"But what no-one has said so far is who the woman was."

"Aggie Phelps."

"Oh, did one of the women in your cell know her?" asked Richenda.

I cursed myself. Usually I am very good at keeping secrets. Fitzroy's threats of what happens to those who breaks the Official Secrets Act are vividly inspirational. If I hadn't been so tired and worn out I would never have let anything slip. I had to cover this up. "It was what someone said when we were held in the first group. I haven't seen her since. It might just have been gossip."

Richenda leant forward, endangering the cake, "Euphemia, this is vital. You must try and recall this woman. At the time you were swept up the chief inspector did not even know of the attack. I had almost convinced him to release you when news of the deaths reached the station. Whoever knew the identity of this woman must have known about the attack!"

In desperation I tried a different tack. "I am sure this is all going to be dangerous. Hans would disapprove of you involving yourself."

Richenda bridled. "The whole reasoning behind our Movement is that women are equal to men. Hans would not dare tell me what to do. Besides, he believes I am already on my way home."

"In all seriousness, Richenda, what could you do?"

"I don't know," snapped Richenda. "What would you do if you were free?"

I looked into Richenda's tired face. Her hair was coming down and in the unflattering light of the early dawn she looked grey, haggard, and ten years older than her actual age. It occurred to me, much as I imagine lightning strikes a rod, that for the first time in her life she was feeling guilty in her actions towards me. Perhaps this was even the first time she had ever felt guilt. Richenda had mellowed magnificently since she had married Hans, and even more since adopting Amy.

Who was I to deny her the opportunity of further emotional growth?[1]

"I would," I said slowly, a plan forming in my mind, "contact any of the other sisters I knew and attempt to find out what I could about Aggie Phelps. It may be she was the firebomber and was accidentally caught up in her plans. If she was I am sure there will be rumours of her involvement in the more militant side of the movement."

"Wait," said Richenda, "are you suggesting she might have been murdered too?"

I shook my head. "I don't know. The key is finding out what Aggie was like. If we can find out about her maybe we can work out why she was in a First Class carriage at the railway station rather than on the march."

"I take it she wasn't a woman of substance?"

"I haven't heard anything about her to suggest she was other than a working woman," I said. I was warming to this plan, but I felt divulging the information Fitzroy had given me about her place of work would be crossing a line too far in the spy's eyes. I had no idea how many women in the movement Richenda knew. She certainly had not been inviting them to dinner at the Muller Estate, but maybe she could root out some rumours. Fitzroy was good with rumours. "You've never heard of a Martha Lake, have you?" I asked.

---

[1] When she had been under the sway of her twin she had been a truly disagreeable and self-centred individual.

82

Richenda shook her head. "Why?"

"She's in the cell with me and I don't think that's her real name. She has . . . " I sought for a generous phrase, "breeding."

"Snotty cow, you mean?"

I gave a slight smile. "That may be one way of describing her. All of us are finding the situation difficult, but she seems totally unprepared for the unpleasantness of prison."

Richenda lowered her eyes. "I had read the accounts of women imprisoned, but if I am honest I thought it exaggerated. And goodness knows, we have suffered very little of what I have read, and yet it was — awful. The attitudes of the men. The treatment." She reached out a hand to me. "I am so sorry I got you involved, Euphemia. I should have told you where we were going." Then her gaze turned steely. "But I will tell you this: after what I have seen and experienced this day I am more committed to the cause than ever before. I only joined the Sisterhood to annoy Richard and our father, but now I see how very much needed it is. How this is a war that must be won. How far the patriarchy will go to discredit us, to humiliate and belittle us, is incredible. I would go so far as to suggest that a man might even have planned that firebombing to discredit the movement!"

I blinked slightly at that. It was a thought that had not occurred to me, and it was without doubt worth passing on to Fitzroy.

There came a loud bang on the door and it was flung wide open. The hateful sergeant who had brought me down stood in the doorway. "Time's up!" I got up before he could manhandle me. Richenda passed me the box. "What's that?" shouted the man in blue. His hand went to his whistle.

"It's a cake," said Richenda quickly. "It's already been examined."

The sergeant came over and peered into the box. "And very nice it looks too. Go down nice with a cup of tea that will. The boys will appreciate it."

"But I brought it for Euphemia. The chief constable . . . "

"The chief is tucked up nice and snug in his bed. So in his absence I am in charge and I say that this is the kind of cake that cannot be allowed. It will excite the women and make them even more difficult. It is the kind of cake that causes hysteria."

Richenda opened her mouth to object.

"Of course any objection she raises you will decry as her being hysterical, I suppose," I interjected.

The sergeant gave me an unpleasant grin. "Ah, *now*, see. You're beginning to understand the system. If you behave proper than you'll be treated right. Meek and mild. That's what I tell my daughters. That's what any man wants to see in a woman."

I stepped towards the door, trying with all my might to send a warning glance to Richenda. "Remember to give my love to Aggie," I said. I could see Richenda struggling with herself. Her natural reaction was to hit this obnoxious man with anything to hand, in this case most likely a chair, but that would only end up with her back inside.[1] She took a deep breath, inflating her person to magnificent proportions, and nodded to me. The sergeant, taking the nod as capitulation, swept up the box under his arm and prodded me in the back with his truncheon. "Get along now. You know the way."

It was with a sense of weary familiarity that I re-entered the cell. The three brick walls and the front of bars had taken on a different aspect now I feared I might need to remain her for some time.

The light coming into the room had grown stronger, and more of the women were waking. From the way they stretched and grimaced I knew they had found the accommodation no more comfortable than I. Eunice and Jasmine, looking like a pair of animate bookends, stood face to face as they tidied each other's hair. Constance was crying quietly with Mary trying to comfort her. Then my gaze alighted on Maisie. She was still curled on the floor. Something about the way she lay struck me as amiss, but I couldn't quite tell what it was. A sense of deep unease crept over me. "Goodness," said the woman Mary had pointed out as Angela Blackwood, "to be so young you can sleep anywhere. I don't feel as if my back will ever be straight again."

I pushed Angela aside and strode quickly across, but even before I laid my hand on her icy forehead I knew Maisie Dawson was dead.

---

[1] Criminal terminology was coming to me with alarming ease.

CHAPTER
THIRTEEN

Fitzroy fumes

"How the hell did this happen?" yelled Fitzroy.

"I don't know," I said quietly. "I wasn't there." We were back in the small room where we had such a pleasant dinner previously. This time there wasn't so much as a sniff of a salt cellar. Fitzroy fixed me with a blazing gaze, "And you were where exactly?"

"In an interview room with Richenda Stapleford. She'd brought me cake." I could have bitten out my tongue the moment I said it. If I had thought Fitzroy was in a temper previously, he was now raging. He span away from me, and picking up a chair, threw it against the wall with such force that it splintered. I almost managed to suppress my scream.[1]

My involuntary sound drew his attention and he turned to face me. I did my best not to shake in my shoes.

"Of course, I will have to remove you from the situation now," he said, his voice flat and cold.

"What do you mean?" I asked with trepidation. "Remove" could mean many things where Fitzroy was concerned.

---

[1] My cry came out as the sort of noise a parrot might make while being strangled.

He took several paces towards me, so I was forced to look up into his face. My instinct was to turn and run, but I knew the door was locked. I was also sure that turning my back on the spy in a bad mood could be ruinous to one's health.

"Do you think I would hurt you?" he asked, his tone now even, but so close to me I could feel his breath on my face.

I swallowed. "If you thought it necessary." I said in as quiet and dignified a manner as I could, and I was relieved my voice hadn't come out like a mouse's squeak. I certainly felt like a tiny rodent being hovered over by a hawk.

He stepped back a pace and laughed. "Ever the realist, Euphemia."

"*Is* it necessary?" I persisted, hopeful now his mood had lightened.

"No. And believe me that even if it were I would always exhaust all other options first." He gave me a flash of his most charming smile. "Not something I would do for everyone."

"So what did you mean by remove me?"

Fitzroy sighed. "Even I am not so callous as to put you back in a cell where a woman has already murdered."

"You think . . .?"

"If a guard had entered, one of you would have awoken. None of the women when interviewed recall anything untoward."

"No one woke when I was taken out," I said.

"But he did not enter, did he? He did not have to make his way amongst you. Besides, we cannot even be sure she was not already dead. Did you notice her?

"No," I said. "I am deeply sorry to say I did not." A thought struck me. "Could they all be involved?"

"It's not a bad thought," answered Fitzroy. "But if they were I suspect you would also be dead. No, this murder was committed by someone desperate enough to kill when locked in a cell with eight other sleeping women, any of whom might have awoken at any time."

"They must be very desperate indeed," I agreed. "But why Maisie? She was the quietest thing."

"The obvious conclusion is that she knew something that the murderer could not allow the police to discover. Did she strike you as bright?"

"Not especially."

"Then it must have been something she saw." He sighed. "She may not even have realised that she saw something of importance."

"But it was something so serious that she had to die."

Fitzroy nodded. "It only goes to confirm my suspicions that one of the women in that cell was involved in the firebombing that killed Wilks. Perhaps even arranged it."

"Could one of them have done it? I don't know London at all well, but did the march go near enough the station for it to happen?"

"Yes, but we have no eyewitnesses that saw anything untoward."

"It's another reckless act," I said. "I assume a London station is very busy at all times?"

Fitzroy nodded again, pursing his lips together. "I don't like it. A nice, cruel, calculating murder I can manage, but this is more . . . "

"If you say hysterical I shall pick up what is left of that chair and hit you with it."

Fitzroy gave a smile of genuine amusement. "No, I am well aware that both men and women can feel themselves so driven into a corner that they will take desperate action. Desperation is unpredictable, and depending on the resources at one's disposal, when panic sets in real disaster can strike."

"There have already been three deaths," I said drily.

"Civil unrest could cause many more," said Fitzroy grimly. "If the individual behind this has a bigger plan, something they are desperate to protect, then I am greatly troubled."

"I see," I said quietly. "Then there is only one course of action to be taken."

I was again shown into a little interview room. There, not sitting at the small table but pacing backwards and forwards, his hat twisting between his hands, was Bertram. On sight of me he dropped his hat and rushed forward to take my hands in his. I trembled slightly at this enthusiasm. Bertram has a habit of wanting to rescue me from situations to the point that he has even offered to marry me. However since his last proposal he has fallen in love again at least once, so I was hopeful I would not have to refuse him again today. My events of the morning had taken their toll on me and I doubted I would have the energy to handle such a situation with the delicacy Bertram required. We are friends, but we do argue a lot.[1]

"My dear Euphemia," he said with a look of such sympathy you would think I had suffered a family bereavement. "I feel I must apologise endlessly for what my wretched sister has embroiled you in."

"Please don't," I said with feeling. "It was extremely foolish of me not to realise what Richenda was up to. The dress. The sudden desire to visit London. I should have been more suspicious."

"At least after this dreadful incident they will have to release you all. No suffragette has ever died in custody before. The newspapers are going to go wild."

"Is that what they are saying?" I asked. "That she suffered police brutality and died?"

"Well, there's nothing in the papers yet. One of the policemen — someone of rank by his strange uniform I should think — told me while I was waiting for you that one of your cellmates had died. He asked me not to repeat it. Said something about my understanding and you would explain?" His eyebrows rose. "You haven't killed anyone, have you, Euphemia?"

"Shall we sit down?" He pulled out a chair for me and I continued. "No, Bertram, I haven't killed anyone.

---

[1] I still do not fit correctly into his well-ordered world, and for all I believe he has some affection for me, this irks him remarkably. Or rather, I irk him often.

90

In fact I am a little offended that you would ask that of me."

"I knew it would have been in self-defence anyway," offered Bertram. I tried very hard not to be proud that he thought I was capable of such a thing.

"No, it's both worse and more complicated than that. You see, I do have to go back into the cell with the murderess. Or rather, I want to. It's become necessary."

CHAPTER
FOURTEEN

Bertram blusters

It took me quite some time to calm Bertram down, but as he has also signed this new-fangled thing called The Official Secrets Act[1] it meant I could reveal everything that had happened so far.

"Fitzroy," said Bertram, as if the word were poison in his mouth. "Hasn't that man caused us enough trouble?"

"But if I hadn't gone out to see Richenda I might have been able to prevent Maisie's death. You must understand I feel culpable."

"Oh, I know that dratted man is more than capable of making you feel like that."

"No, he wanted to remove me from the situation. I had to beg to stay."

"Good God, woman, do you want to be murdered?"

"I was talking with Richenda about cake when it happened." Bertram looked baffled. "She came to see me. I wasn't in the cell when the murder occurred. I am almost certain I would have awoken otherwise."

---

[1] Only a man could have come up with a name like that. It sounds terribly schoolboyish to me.

"I suppose that does make it less likely the murderer will be concerned with you," interrupted Bertram. "It's not like you could have seen anything."

"But that's just it," I said, feeling tears prickle my eyes, "if I had been there maybe I would have been able to do something . . . "

"Like getting killed?" snapped Bertram.

"If I had kept my eyes open. Paid more attention. She was so young, Bertram!"

Bertram reached out a hand to me across the table and patted mine. "You can't think like that, Euphemia," he said gruffly. "We both know better than most there is evil in this world and there are ones intent on it whether we will or no."

"But . . . "

"Enough," said Bertram, tapping my hand lightly and withdrawing his own.[1] "I see that nothing I say will deter you from your course and frankly, if Fitzroy wants to keep you in that cell I'm not entirely sure what I can do about that without striking the cad. Not that I wouldn't, if I needed to," he added.

I gave a faint smile. "That will not be necessary. Although I was technically absent when the murder was likely committed until a doctor has been able to determine, by which I mean guess, the time of death, I must still be a suspect and it would be awkward for all concerned if I was removed from the scene." I put my head on one side, musing. "I imagine that Fitzroy is

---

[1] This appeared to be closest he dared to slapping my hand. In some ways Bertram is surprisingly wise.

currently engaged in checking whether or not I had any connection with Maisie."

"Good God! You think he would suspect you?"

"He is thorough. Besides, even you asked me."

Bertram made a number of gruffling sounds like a bear hunting for honey, which I took to be an apology.[1]

Finally he said, "What can I do?"

A glimmer of an idea formed at the back of my mind. I already had Richenda out in the field, as it were, researching matters I could not attend to inside my cell, so why not use Bertram as well? But I knew the task I would set for Bertram would be far less to his taste. "The man who died in the fire, Wilks, was a member of some elite — er — clubs. If I can get from Fitzroy the name of his favourite haunts perhaps you could be so good as to investigate and see how he is remembered?"

Bertram brightened at that. "That certainly sounds like something I could do. I would be happy to help."

I felt certain that Bertram's mood would change when he learnt the true nature of clubs I wished him to investigate.

We parted on good terms and I returned to the cell, feeling weary and so nervy I was wide awake. Again I was escorted by the sergeant, who was overly keen on restraint. As he passed a fellow guard I heard him

---

[1] I am of course imagining what a bear would sound like. I have yet to meet one. Although my life has thus far proved so unpredictable that I am not ruling out encountering a bear one day.

hailed as "Givens". It was a name I intended to mention to Fitzroy should he show any sign of wanting someone to expend his ire upon. The man was a beast. Not only for the names he called me — he had left bruises on my upper arms that were quite unnecessary as I was not resisting.

The mood in the cell was sombre. Sergeant Givens thrust me forward, but did not then leave. "Right, *ladies*, your stockings. Let's be having them." As one the women in the cell turned towards him. I imagine each of us looking as astonished as the other. I could not see for I too was staring open mouthed at the sergeant. His lips curved into a sneering smile. "Or do you need any help?" he asked.

"Outrageous," came the clear, sharp tones of the woman I now knew to be Martha Lake.

I heard the sound of skirts rustling and turned to see that Mary Hill, her back now turned towards the sergeant, was obeying his orders.

"You can't ask us for 'em!" growled Abigail Stokes, as vicious as any tiger in an Indian jungle.[1]

"Yes, I bleedin' can," retorted the Sergeant. "Should have been taken off you when you were taken in, but what with you lot murdering each other it got forgot."

---

[1] Not that I have ever been to India, but I can imagine. Stapleford Hall had a rug that was once a tiger and still displayed quite daunting teeth and claws. I used to dream it had awakened and was stalking the house looking for people to eat. When I told Merry, she said she would leave a trail of breadcrumbs from it to Richard Stapleford's study just in case.

"Murder!" said Constance. "I thought that poor young woman had died of natural causes."

"Yeah, that's right. One goes blue in the face from *natural* causes," said the hateful sergeant, mimicking her. "Choked, she was, and our doc reckons a stocking would just about do it."

"It really is better just to give him what he asks," said Mary, holding her now-removed stockings out to the sergeant. I saw they were badly torn. "He will only fetch reinforcements to carry out his orders if we refuse."

"Nonsense," said Martha. "The man is a pervert."

The sergeant raised his truncheon menacingly.

"That is as may be," said Mary calmly, "but he is right. A murder has been committed and we must do what we can to find the fiend who did this to our poor fallen sister."

With varying degrees of awkwardness, and many muttered comments, finally all the women had divested themselves of their stockings and handed them over. The sergeant bundled them all together in one big pile. Then he clanged the door shut and locked it.

"Wait a minute," I called out. "How will you know whose is whose?"

"Doesn't matter, does it?" he replied with a leer. "I reckons how you was all in it together, so you'll all hang." Then he stomped off.

"What does he mean, all hang?" asked Jasmine Pettigrew in a wavering voice.

"Now, now, dear, don't let the nasty man upset you," answered her sister.

"I reckon the stupid man is only trying to frighten us," said Martha haughtily. "As Miss . . . " she looked at me.

"St John," I supplied.

"As Miss St John remarked, the man has no way of telling one stocking from another."

"I reckon he was doin' it for a bet with the lads," broke in Abigail. "Who can get the underthings off a suffragette! You know the kind of thing."

"Well, really," said Martha, turning away in disgust.

"Was she strangled?" asked Constance, the doctor's wife. "I would have thought . . . " she tailed off.

"It was still dark and the body was removed quickly," said Mary. "I think all of us were too shocked to take notice of the details."

"I mean, if she had been hanged," continued Constance, "I mean, hanged herself, then it would have been obvious by the colouring, but strangled, I am unsure . . . "

Jasmine Pettigrew sat down heavily on the bench all the colour draining from her face. "Have some thought for others," snapped her sister, Eunice. "My poor sister is prone to fainting fits."

"Undo her stays, then," said Abigail, not too unkindly. "They are an unnatural harness for any woman and you two seem to have right pulled yours in."

"Eunice," moaned Jasmine, "is that gal mentioning *underthings*?"

"Too right I am," said Abigail. "Next thing you know that copper'll be checking to see all our laces are intact."

Jasmine gave a low moan at this and slid onto the floor, her eyes fluttering. Her sister fussed over her. "Now see what you have done, you unnatural creature," she cried.

"I have smelling salts in my reticule — oh, blast it. They took that away," said Martha. "Fan her face."

"With what?" said Abigail as Eunice flapped her hands uselessly around her sister's face. "Undo her stays, you silly besom. There's no way she should have slept in something that tight. It's a wonder there's any blood left in her head."

"Allow me," said Constance. She turned Jasmine on her side and then quickly and efficiently loosened her stays. Gradually the colour came back to Jasmine's face. Constance helped her sit up slowly and demanded someone find her a glass of water.

I found some water in a forgotten mug and passed it to her. "Did you learn about this sort of thing from your husband?" I asked, impressed.

Constance nodded. "I asked him for information on the sort of injuries that one might expect to find after a march."

"He does not mind you attending?" asked Martha.

"Of course not," said Constance. "He says that in another time I would have had the brains to be a doctor myself."

"What a forward-thinking man," said Martha in somewhat shocked tones.

"There are women who have qualified as doctors, I believe," said Mary. "A very few indeed. Of course they are not generally allowed to practise."

"Then what the hell is the bleedin' point?" asked Abigail.

"Why, to show the men they are capable," said Mary. "Just as I have taken degree examinations, but will never be awarded a degree in my lifetime, despite my excellent marks."

"I do believe the female brain, while smaller, makes many more internal connections than the male, and thus leads to a superior intelligence when correctly trained." Angela Blackwood spoke for the first time. "I am an amateur, but extremely keen, anatomist and botanist. Angela Blackwood. You may have heard of me."

CHAPTER
FIFTEEN

Introductions

"I am afraid I did not know." Mary was the first to recover. "It is not my field of speciality."

"Yes, I heard you say you were an academic," said Angela brusquely. "Never wanted to have a man sanctioning my learning."

"The college I attended was entirely staffed by women," said Mary calmly.

"Bet they were all appointed by men. All their learning would come from books written by men. I make up my own mind."

"But you cannot disregard the accumulated knowledge of all those who have gone before us," said Mary, astonished.

"Don't see why not," snapped Angela. "A sharp knife and a dead rabbit will teach me as much as any anatomy book."

"But not of human anatomy," I pointed out.

"Yes, well, I'm wearing one, aren't I?" She waggled a long finger at us, and I could not help noticing the fingernail was ragged and especially dirty.

"How extraordinary," exclaimed Martha, putting into words what we were doubtless all thinking; then she added, none too quietly, "She must be quite mad."

"Doubtless I would be considered so by some," answered Angela, "but for me the world is full of the insane and I am among the few to notice."

"As an anatomist," I ventured, "do you have any views on how a young woman might be strangled silently with a stocking?"

Angela shrugged. "Easily enough. Tie a knot in the stocking. Get that over the lump you have here in your throat." She thrust out a grimy hand to touch my neck. I managed to force myself not to step back, but I could not repress a wince. "Preferably have her on the front. Knee in the back, cross the stocking, and pull. She wasn't much of a girl. I doubt it would have taken much effort or much time. Of course, the better the stocking the better it would have worked."

"And *how* would you know this?" asked Mary.

Angela tapped the side of her temple. "The application of a little logical thought." She gave a sneer, showing yellowed teeth. "I would have thought a mathematician, of all people, would be able to do some rudimentary deduction."

Jasmine gave a low moan. "Oh, my dear," said Eunice, patting her hand. "Mrs Woodley, do you think she will recover?"

Constance came over and sat beside Jasmine again. She took her wrist in a light grip and closed her eyes. A moment later she commented, "Her pulse is still a little fluttery, but it is quite clearly there."

"If she didn't have one she'd be dead," said Angela sharply. "Any fool can see she's still breathing despite those damn fool things!" She indicated the half-open stays. I had to agree that the Pettigrew sisters, perhaps in deference to their age and experience, were among the most tightly laced women I have ever beheld. "Never wear underthings myself. Much better to let nature do its work and have a fresh flow of air round there!"

Jasmine, who had opened her eyes at this extraordinary speech, gave a little cry and slumped back down on the floor.

"Playacting," muttered Angela, none too quietly. I felt she had a point, but I was aware I would make myself extremely unpopular if I sided with her. As it was my frequent trips away from the cell would surely have aroused suspicions. And as if on cue, Abigail Stokes rounded on me. "Where you been gadding off to again?" she snarled. "You a coppers' nark?"

"Is there anything in particular you are worried about me narking about?" I countered. I sensed with Abigail one needed to give as good as one got.

"You saying I'm a murderer?" growled Abigail.

"It appears one of us is," said Mary calmly.

"Yeah, that's as may be, but I want to know if Lady High-and-Mighty here is accusing me."

"I am accusing no one," I said as icily as I could, "and I am hardly high and mighty. I am the paid companion of Richenda Muller."

"A German?" asked Abigail. She spat on the floor. "Bloody Germans."

"We have met some very nice German people on our walking holidays," said Eunice suddenly. "A most tidy and correct people."

"Lovely table manners," added Jasmine weakly.

"Oh, Jasmine," cried Eunice. She and Constance helped Jasmine to sit up.

"Perhaps," said Mary, "it might help if we shared a little of ourselves with each other."

"What good would that do?" demanded Angela, "The murderess is bound to lie."

"But the others will tell the truth," I countered.

"Think you'll be able to tell the difference?" asked Angela. "It seems to me that even those of you who are supposedly trained in the ways of analysis have exceptionally poor skills."

"I think it would be a good idea," said Constance. "If we all work together perhaps we will be able to expose the killer in our midst."

Jasmine gave another little moan at this. Constance gave her a sideways glance and an expression I recognised crossed her face. It was exactly how I felt when Richenda was being particularly tiresome.[1]

"We could start with explaining why we joined the Sisterhood?" suggested Mary. "As I have said I am a trained mathematician, but barred from holding the same degree as my male peers despite proving I am their equal. I feel the injustice between the sexes most keenly."

"As some of you know I am a doctor's wife," said Constance, picking up the thread, "My husband is keen for our son to follow in his footsteps, but it is already

---

[1] That is to say, the recipient of the glance could do with a jolly good slap.

clear to me that my daughter is the brighter of the two. Why should she not enjoy the same opportunities?"

"Because it is our duty to bear sons and daughters for our husbands," cut in Martha Lake.

"Regretting joining the Shrieking Sisterhood, are you?" asked Abigail.

Martha blushed red. "I do not wish to disturb the natural order of things. A woman's role is to raise children for the future of the Empire. It is her whole purpose in life." There was a sharp intake of breath and I saw Eunice's mouth was tightly pursed. Even her fingers had curled into fists. "However," said Martha. She licked her lips. "However, I do see that women are as intelligent as men. Often more so." She gave a short little laugh. "And I think it is right we have a say in the running of things. I believe we should have the vote."

"What about earning our own livings?" burst out Eunice. "It may be alright for those born into the upper classes, or those endowed with such natural graces that they avail themselves of marriage to escape their station, but some of us have little choice. My sister and I cared for elderly father until his death two years ago. He had been respectably in trade, but the early death of our mother in a terrible accident and the ruination of his business by an unscrupulous banker occasioned the loss of his health. For the greater part of our lives my sister and I have supported him through our work as teachers."

"And we were happy to do so," added Jasmine. A tear trickled down her cheek.

"But as impoverished school teachers with a dependent father and, we both own it, no exceptional looks, there was never any prospect of marriage for either of us. Let alone bearing children."

"No indeed," said Jasmine. "But working with them helped, didn't it, dear?"

"Of course, dear," responded Eunice, "we have helped shape the minds of many children. Who knows but that one of them may not do the Empire a great service."

"Or you may have simply helped them grow into decent, moral adults," I said. "That in itself is a worthy life choice."

"Thank you, my dear," said Eunice. "Not everyone appreciates that the natural human animal is one that comes completely uncivilised into the world. Manners may maketh man, but they must be learned."

"Oh, give me strength," muttered Angela.

"I assume your reason for joining the Sisterhood is that you believe men and women are created equal."

"No," snapped Angela. "I believe women are better. In fact I prefer women."

Again there was the sound of intakes of breath while this statement was considered. "Well, I don't," said Abigail firmly. "I like men a lot of the time." She nodded at Martha, "Though I accept a lot of them can be right little bug —" she coughed and corrected herself, "blighters. My mam's mam was a worker in a mill. She was one of twelve. Didn't fancy spending her whole life in the mill, so she ran off to London to make her fortune."

"That would not seem very wise," said Eunice, frowning.

"Nah," said Abigail, "it wasn't, but she didn't have a lot of options, did she? Had even bleedin' less in London. Ended up, like most of you ladies have guessed, walking the streets. That's 'ow I came about." She looked around and seemed to stare at Martha in particular, "but despite how she had to earn her crust, she were a good ma. Determined I wouldn't end up the same way she did. Saved up she did and apprenticed me to a seamstress. Now, I sew gowns for some of the finest in the land. Not that they will ever know it."

"And your mother, dear?" asked Jasmine.

"Dead, I expect. Didn't want me to be associated with what she did — and the seamstress who took me on, only did 'cause Mam overpaid and promised not to hang around me."

"You can't know that," I said.

"Lifespan on the streets ain't that long," said Abigail. "Besides, she'd be too old for the game by now. One of her men or the drink will have done for her."

"Good heavens," I said, "how terrible. She must have been very brave."

Abigail gave me a strange look.

"Very foolish," said Martha. "If she'd stayed in the place God had given her she would have been perfectly safe."

"I take it you have never visited a mill?" asked Constance. Martha reddened further. "Neither have I," continued Constance, "but my husband has been called to attend accidents at one and the stories he has told me would make your blood run cold if I were to repeat them."

"Sounds to me like you lot are of more a load of Bolsheviks than women seeking enfranchisement!" said Angela from the corner, where she had retreated to.

"What about you, coppers' nark?" asked Abigail, but she seemed less angry and more curious.

"I confess I am here by mistake. I foolishly failed to realise my employer's intent, nor why she had dressed me in this fashion." I looked around at seven pairs of eyes that now seemed a lot less friendly. "However, I do support the right of women to have the vote. I believe that many women, like Mary, Eunice, Jasmine, and Constance's daughter, are capable of great intellectual feats and that we are denied our rightful place in what we call civilised society."

"And exactly how do you support the cause?" asked Abigail.

"I am forthright in my views," I said.

"But you don't march or give public speeches?"

I shook my head. "Until today those opportunities have been denied to me. Generally we live quite quietly in the country."

"Well that's got us a lot further forward, hasn't it?" said Angela sarcastically.

I did not respond, but in my heart I agreed with her. I felt we had come no nearer to finding who was the murderess in our midst and the thought of spending another night in this cell filled me with horror.

CHAPTER
SIXTEEN

Fitzroy frets

It is difficult to tell the time when incarcerated. Time stretches and overfills one's attention. After the bout of exchanges between us, the women again lapsed into silence. Eunice and Jasmine whispered quietly to one another from time to time. And when the guard came past us at what I imagined was luncheon time to inflict upon us yet more stale bread, this time accompanied by a hard-rinded cheese that was well beyond its best, they did their best to convince the young guard that they required the return of their knitting bag, which remarkably they had brought upon their trip with them to the march.

"You never know when you will able to snatch a moment," Eunice had explained.

"My sister and I are avid knitters," contributed Jasmine.

"We were raised never to be idle," interjected Eunice. I thought for one remarkable moment that the guard would cave under their onslaught. He could not have been more than two and, twenty, and sported eight or nine hairs proudly on his upper lip. He was polite and it was clear that dealing with what might otherwise have been considered "ladies" he felt quite unsuited to deal with their various demands. He had also most foolishly stepped inside the cell rather than shoving the food in and escaping as the others had done. Now, he was caught between the two sisters, who hovered mere inches from his person. Sweat beaded on his forehead and I felt a little sorry for him. Though not sorry enough to intervene.

"Poor boy," said Mary quietly at my side. "Should we rescue him?"

"He should be ashamed of supporting the harassment of women," I retorted loud enough to see the tops of his ears glow red.

"I imagine he needs to keep his job," said Mary. "Not all of us are lucky enough to enjoy a private income."

Stung by her words, I snapped, "I have been quite clear that I am a paid companion."

"I was referring to myself," said Mary calmly. She tilted her head to one side, "It must have occurred to you that I was fortunate in my circumstances. One does need to pay for university tuition, regardless of whether one is awarded a degree."

Now it was my turn to blush. Mary's manners were those of a woman gently bred, but the surname she had given me was a most ordinary one. I had also gained the impression that she was unwed. She certainly wore no ring on her finger. Of course I had no way of verifying anything that any of these ladies claimed without resorting to Fitzroy, but the back of my neck was tingling and I had begun to suspect that Mary Hill harboured more than one mystery.

"Ah, they have let him go," said the object of my attention. I turned to see the guard now on the other side of the cell door, locking it behind him. The expression on his face was one of unguarded relief. Eunice and Jasmine retired to their favourite spot on the bench and commenced whispering to one another again. "I must confess to being somewhat relieved that he appears to have denied their request," said Mary, so softly that I could barely hear her. "The thought of knitting needles among us in the cell when we have already had one death would, to me, not be conducive of a decent night's sleep."

"You mean they could be used as a weapon," I responded shocked. "You think Eunice and Jasmine . . ."

"My dear, at this point I suspect everyone," said Mary. "I am convinced that poor little Maisie would not have harmed a fly. I cannot conceive of a reason for her to be killed unless one of our cellmates harbours some unnatural tendencies or an affliction of brainstorms."

It was with these ominous words still echoing in my brain that I entered the room where Fitzroy awaited me. It appeared he shared my concerns, for I had been summoned once again. The doctor awaited to check my injury and once more a civilised meal awaited me. Fitzroy and I ate in silence. I was preoccupied with my own thoughts and the spy seemed intent on watching me closely. I therefore took the only option open to me inside a locked room and ignored him completely.

When we had finished, never a stickler for convention, he poured me a cup of coffee himself. "Are you still determined to stay in the cell overnight?"

"I cannot say I am looking forward to the experience, but I feel it is my duty."

"I warn you, Euphemia, this is your last chance. I will from now only remove you from the situation if you expressly ask. I have wasted more than enough time on this point."

"I have not asked you to keep pestering me with the same question," I responded, snappily, for my head still ached.

A spark flashed in Fitzroy's eyes. He took a moment before he responded. "You are fortunate you are not officially on our staff. I do not suffer insolence from subordinates."

"I am most definitely not a member of your staff," I said flatly. "I am . . . " I trailed off. I did not have any idea of what I was. A smile played across Fitzroy's lips as he followed my train of thought. "You are an amateur," he said.

I was tempted to enquire as to more precisely I was an "amateur" at, but he had annoyed me. "I am indeed an amateur," I said coldly. "How very galling it must be to owe your last rescue to an amateur." I stressed the last two words.

But instead of rising to my bait, he nodded briefly. "You had a little help blowing that wall up. Although if you had looked at it as you are looking at me now, I would not have been surprised if it had crumbled under your gaze."

I sighed. "True."

"Come, Euphemia, let us cease this quarrelling. Neither of us are in the best of health. I will forbear asking you again if you wish to leave." He took a sip of his coffee and said with a casualness that I did not believe for a moment, "Did you mention my presence to Bertram?"

"Yes. He has signed the Official Secrets Act, after all."

"Hmm. Did you have a reason other than mere friendliness?"

"I thought if you gave me the name of the clubs Wilks used to frequent he might be able to discover something of help."

Fortunately[1] Fitzroy had swallowed just before my comment. However, his eyebrows shot up almost into his hairline. "You want to send Bertram into a bordello?"

"You did say it was a higher class of establishment."

Fitzroy threw back his head and laughed. "Do you think Bertram is in the habit of frequenting such places?" he asked.

I felt myself begin to blush. I knew that gentleman did — well, that they *saw* certain women for entertainment, but I had never considered Bertram in that light. I found that even edging close to the thought made me most uncomfortable. So I snapped back at him, "Doubtless you would be more at home in such

---

[1] Or unfortunately, depending on your perspective.

establishments, but, as you say, you are not currently in the best of health."

Fitzroy put down his coffee cup and leaned across the table. "I assure you I am well enough."

I flinched backwards. He gave a slight smile and also sat back. "It is not a bad idea if he doesn't make a hash of it. He will have to be willing to play his part to the — shall we say — hilt. You may tell him that Wilks's favoured establishment was The Gilded Lily."

"Which is where?" I asked coldly.

"I have no intention of telling you. I do not trust you not to visit there yourself — either to think to 'save' the inhabitants or from idle curiosity." I bridled angrily, but he continued, "Any of the porters at the gentleman's clubs in the city will be able to direct him."

I took a breath. It was better to have it all out in the open. "I have also asked Richenda to help."

"What?" He made the single word as sharp as an arrow.

"I have of course told her nothing of your involvement . . . "

"You do still have a modicum of self-preservation then."

"But I thought she could use her contacts to attempt to discover more about the woman who died in the carriage."

Fitzroy shrugged. "I doubt her husband will let her investigate, but it isn't that bad an idea." He gave me one of his most mocking smiles. "Quite the little team you are gathering around you. You will be after my position next."

"Oh, I could never be like you," I said sweetly.

Fitzroy frowned. "Much as I am enjoying this tete-a-tete, do you have anything of significance to tell me?"

"Martha Lake is in all likelihood using an alias."

"We had worked that out," said Fitzroy with a sigh. "Even my staff have some level of competence. We have checked the backgrounds of all the women with you, and Martha Lake does not exist. However, that does not make her a murderess, rather a woman likely attempting to shield her name. I had set in motion discreet enquires to see if a woman of her age and quality is known to be missing. Your observations should be of the more detailed kind as only a close proximity can produce."

"Eunice and Jasmine Pettigrew did their best to persuade a guard to allow them their knitting."

"I suppose if two were involved it would make things much easier, but if they were that clever would they draw attention to themselves by asking for a weapon?"

"Killing someone by strangulation is, as you pointed out, very risky," I answered. "And it would be easy to claim that someone else had stolen the needle from them."

"But why would they want to kill again?"

"I did think of hinting I had seen something last night."

"A very last resort, I would suggest," said Fitzroy, "and only when I have my men to hand. Your murder would be very inconvenient."

"I would not enjoy it much myself," I said. "It was a foolish idea. Although Abigail Stokes is of the opinion that I am some kind of 'coppers' nark' — I think that was it — and it didn't sound good for my health."

"Hmm."

"Constance Woodley is a deeply motivated suffragette and as a doctor's wife may have knowledge of the human anatomy. However, Angela Blackwood is an extreme oddity. Some kind of amateur scientist. She was the one who told us how Maisie must have been killed. She is extremely anti-social."

"You think her the strongest possibility?"

"Quite the opposite. Why would she draw such attention to herself if she was guilty? I do not believe her to be mad, though, but simply eccentric. Mary Hill, on the other hand, is a woman with secrets, but so far her nature has not seemed to me consistent with one who could kill without at least showing remorse."

"That may be what we have to wait for," said Fitzroy slowly.

I nodded. "You mean that will all of us locked up together with no immediate chance of release the murderess will grow desperate. How long can you keep us locked away?"

Fitzroy shrugged. "Not very much longer, I should think. The story is now in the newspapers. Although we have managed to ensure most of the details are inaccurate."

"I see," I said.

Fitzroy eyed me with obvious misgiving. "What are you planning to do, Euphemia?"

I looked him square in the face and said, "Nothing you would not do, Eric."

I had the pleasure of seeing the spy pale ever so slightly.

As I was escorted back to my cell for the night, I ran back over the conversation in my mind. I was certain there were questions I had forgotten to ask and things I had forgotten to say, but I did relish the experience that I had unsettled Fitzroy, even if only a little. If nothing else such self-satisfaction was a useful distraction from the worry of the long night ahead. During which I would be sleeping no more than six feet from a cold-blooded murderess.

CHAPTER
SEVENTEEN

Fights and weaponry

I have never been more grateful to open my eyes to sunlight. I sat up at once and mentally did a head count of the women in the cell. It was bright enough for me to assure myself that all of them were either awake or breathing as they slept. Certainly no one was lying in a crumpled heap in any of the corners. I encountered an unfriendly gaze from Abigail Stokes and my back spasmed alarmingly, causing me to utter an "oof" rather like my mother's old spaniel in its declining years.[1]

"Awake, are you, coppers' nark?"

"Your insult would have more effect if I understood what a nark was," I said coolly. My sleeping accommodation had not placed me in a social mood. My head itched and my hair was in dire need of a wash.[2] I felt at a loss to deal with the situation and

---

[1] They say that pets take after their owners and Mother's spaniel, Walter, had been grumpy and nippy with a very shrill bark. I was not terribly sad when it died after being crushed by a cow whose legs it had been snapping at.

[2] As was the rest of me, but that is perhaps a little too indelicate to mention.

frankly both bored and terrified. In short I was not brimming with Christian kindness.

"I mean you're a spy for the coppers."

"And by coppers I assume you mean the policemen who have thrown me in and out of this cell with such tender care?"

"Are you daft or what?"

"So I am a daft spy? That would seem to be a most unlikely combination."

"Ladies, please," said Mary in her quiet voice. "We are all in this together."

A spark of indignation arose in my breast. Mary was continually calm and acquiescent. She advocated harmony at all times, and I for one, was being to find it all rather galling. I blushed, wondering if it was because I normally found myself being the voice of reason and did not like to have my position usurped. Then it occurred to me that if we all continued being calm and harmonious, how on earth was I to discover anything? It might only be when harsh words were spoken and emotions roused that the truth might slip out. I took a deep breath and prepared to be as difficult as my mother has ever thought me.

"There is a saying, though I doubt you would know it, Miss Stokes, about protesting too much. You seem most vocal about the possibility of a spy among us. I am forced to ask myself if you are intent on drawing attention away from yourself."

"Why, you bleedin' . . . " began Abigail, but I raised my voice above hers, employing the perfect vowels my mother had bestowed on me and which I had been at such pains to conceal from my employers. "I'd have thought that anyone with any sense at all would think that discovering who was the murderess among us was far more important than whether someone was a spy? Unless you believe the spy is trying to uncover the murderess and that is something you do not wish to come to pass."

Abigail Stokes opened and closed her mouth a few times. Her face turned beetroot. "Are you calling me a bleedin' killer now?" she fairly screamed at me.

"The only person I am certain is not the killer is myself," I said calmly, in the full knowledge that not rising to her ire would incense her further.

"Why you . . . " Her face contorted fury and she leapt for me. As she did so I saw her shake something from her sleeve. I had a momentary glimpse of a flash of silver. I dived to one side, not caring that I must throw myself with force onto the ground, and rolled to one side immediately as I was sure she would launch herself at me. However, the attack did not come. Instead I looked up to see Eunice and Jasmine very effectively holding Abigail mid-flight in a most secure armlock.

"Sadly, the village children we taught were not always raised by their parents as one might hope," said Eunice.

"Indeed," echoed her sister in her fainter voice, "at times one was forced to be most unladylike with the older boys."

Mary walked over to Abigail who was spitting furious obscenities and twisted the fingers of one of her hands in an expert manner. "A difficult male cousin," she said shortly. "Always trying to put unpleasant things down my back. One learns to intercept."

From my position on the floor it struck me that these three women were far more physically capable than I had assumed. The unwelcome thought exploded in my brain that perhaps Maisie had been killed by more than one person. As I got shakily to my feet, and saw the intense interest of the women who had not so far been involved in this situation, I had the horrendous thought that perhaps they were all involved.

Angela Blackwood came across to Mary and they bent their heads over whatever Mary had wrested from Abigail. "Why," said Angela," she's made herself a shank."

Constance stood up from her seat on the bench. "What is that?"

Mary turned the glinting thing over in her hands. "A crude knife," she said.

Constance's hands flew to her face in alarm. "Wherever did she get such a thing?"

"Looks like a spoon she's been sharpening on the wall," said Angela. "I've heard of such things. It's an old prisoner's trick." She brought her face close to the restrained Abigail. "I'm thinking that this woman hasn't been that open about her past. I'm thinking she's not a stranger to being in a cell, and I doubt she was incarcerated for being a suffragette."

"If that were the case," said Mary slowly, "then perhaps Euphemia's accusation has merit."

"You mean she could have done a deal to spy on the Sisterhood," said Constance, her voice shaking. "Surely no sister could do that to another?"

Martha Lake, who had edged as far away as she could into the corner when the action had begun, now spoke in her well-bred voice, "Whether or not that is the case, it appears we have uncovered a woman with a tendency towards violence. I think, ladies, I should call the guard, we appear to have discovered our murderess."

"Though so far they have shown themselves to be very uncouth young men," said Eunice, tightening her grip on Abigail, "I think that might be a very good idea."

"But, sister," said Jasmine, "Miss Dawson was strangled, not stabbed."

"No, the stabbing was for whoever she had next in mind," said Angela. "It would take a while to sharpen a spoon against the wall. Stupid of the constabulary not to give us wooden ones."

"And not to count them when they were removed from the cell," added Martha. "It must have been that very young man."

"I wasn't the one asking for bleedin' knitting needles," said Abigail. She was no longer struggling against the Pettigrew sisters. I detected a note of fear in her voice. "That little girl was killed by someone strong. And these two biddies are fair twisting my arms out of their sockets."

"Why did you fashion a knife for yourself?" I asked.

"Self-protection," snapped Abigail. "As you all keep saying, one of us is a bleedin' killer. And she knows a thing or two herself," she nodded at Mary. "Fair broke my fingers."

An image came immediately of Mary crumbling the almost stone-hard bread into her soup. Whoever killed Maisie would have had to have more than average womanly strength.

"It does not matter what skills are being displayed," cut in Martha. "Only one of us has shown violence towards the others."

"Two!" protested Abigail. "Besides, she provoked me. Can't you see she was trying to start a quarrel?"

"I find that most unlikely," said Martha. "Miss St John speaks and acts with the manners of the well-bred."

I felt a twinge of guilt. I looked more closely at Abigail. She was certainly afraid, but then if everyone in the room had decided to turn on me, I too would be ill at ease. At this moment I found myself only able to rule Constance and Martha out as ones who had not shown any physical prowess. Then again, I would never have suspected that the Pettigrew sisters could have hold such a termagant as Abigail at bay so easily.

"I would be most grateful if we could decide what to do," said Jasmine suddenly. "This is all very tiring. I am not as young as I was when I had to deal with playground situations."

"Glad I didn't go to her school," muttered Angela as she passed me and returned to her seat. "I'll tell you what," she continued. "I have a bit of a gift. I can conduct a séance and we can ask little Maisie who killed her. Victims of violent death do tend to linger."

"What an unpleasant thought," said Jasmine faintly.

"I am summoning the guard," announced Martha. "If nothing else this woman must be removed from the cell. They will surely do so when we hand over the — er — shank."

"No," cried Abigail. "If you do that they'll beat me. Some of them coppers keep chains for use on the suffragettes!"

"Nonsense," said Martha.

"I'm afraid it is true," I said. "One of the guards boasted of the fact to me. Although he said those methods were yet to be employed at this station."

"I should not like anyone to be beaten," said Constance. "Least of all a sister."

"But she is in all likelihood the killer," said Martha. "I can assure you a potential beating will be the least of her worries. She will face the noose."

"And I am sure the constabulary will be very pleased to have the situation cleared up so easily," said Angela. "After all, it seems to me that Miss Stokes is unlikely to have anyone to protest her case. Working-class girl. No better than she should be. That, I imagine, is what the papers will say."

"Oh dear," said Constance. "I cannot condone violence of any sort, but I do fear Miss Blackwood has the right of it. The police will most likely take the easiest path out of this situation."

"Do you not believe in Justice?" I said angrily.

"I most certainly do," said Constance. "But I fear the situation will soon become political. The newspaper men will be making a great deal of this story and the fear for Mr Asquith's government must be that any sympathy towards the Sisterhood may be aroused. Far better to name, shame, and hang one of us for the hysterical murder of another."

"But one of us was killed," answered Martha, a level of exasperation creeping into her voice.

"I reckon my séance is the best way forward," said Angela.

"Nonsense," snapped Martha.

"We have often sensed dear Father's spirit watching over us," said Jasmine unexpectedly.

"That's hardly the same thing," answered her sister. "This woman is talking of raising the dead."

Jasmine paled. "How very unpleasant."

"Complete nonsense," said Martha emphatically.

"Just summon the ruddy guard," said Abigail. "My arms are fair popping out of their sockets."

"Perhaps if we removed the shank," said Constance.

"Are you for trying a séance too?" asked Mary.

"I have no fixed opinion on spiritualism," answered Constance, "but my husband, who has seen people pass away as any doctor in village practice will, is adamant that there is an absence when death encroaches and he is most decidedly a man of science."

"I too have heard some interesting discussion on the subject during my time at the university," said Mary. "What do you think, Euphemia?"

"My experience has been," I said, thinking of Madam Arcana, "that mediums offer a mixture of information some of which may feel true and some of which does not." I nodded to Angela, "I mean no offence, but I fear at best people hear what they wish to hear and at worst they are misled by the unscrupulous."

"As if I could take offence at that," said Angela with a sharp laugh.

"But who would take the shank?" asked Constance.

"If you are insistent that this women be not handed over to the guard, which I consider most unwise, then I will take it," said Martha, and held out her hand.

"I think, perhaps, none of us should have it," said Constance. "I could not feel easy that it was in the cell. It could be obtained by the killer."

"We could throw it out of the cell," I suggested. "If we aim correctly though the bars it will likely go unnoticed for some time in the dim corridor. And even if it is found then no one will be sure where it came from." Abigail threw me a startled look.

"What about fingermarks?" asked Constance nervously. "I hear there is a new science that traces who has touched things by examining the marks on the ends of one's fingers."

"Let 'em try and look at my fingers," said Abigail, "I'll give them a knuckle sandwich."

"No one has taken an imprint of our fingers, which is how I believe the science works," I said. "I read a little about it in the newspapers. I believe we have handled it enough between us that any marks would be quite confused."

"So you too side with this woman?" asked Martha.

"No," I said. "I do not wish to side with anyone. However, I do wish that true justice will take its course, and I have been convinced by all of you that merely turning Miss Stokes over to the guard will ensure her found guilty without the bother of a proper investigation. That is not something my conscience will allow."

"Neither will mine," said Constance stoutly. "Well said, Euphemia."

I could, of course, hope that Fitzroy would see that true justice was done, but I feared that the spy would be most keen on closing the incident at quickly as possible. I had borne first-hand witness to his ruthlessness and I doubted strongly that he considered the death of poor little Maisie Dawson as important. Indeed, I knew he was chafing to be put back in the dark world of intrigue that was his natural milieu. I feared Fitzroy would all too happily embrace the easy option.

"So throw out the knife and we can prepare for the séance," said Angela. Mary went over to the bars and threw the knife into the corridor. It landed some distance from the cell.

"I believe that to be out of reach," she said in a satisfied manner.

Jasmine and Eunice released Abigail, who stood forlornly attempting to rub the feeling back into her sore arms. "Thanks," she said very quietly as I passed her to sit on the bench.

"So let's get on with it," said Eunice stoutly.

"Needs to be twilight, at least," said Angela. "The spirits do not like bright light."

Martha groaned. "How tiresome of them."

As I had seen Madam Arcana take séances during both evening and daylight hours I did not know what to make of this statement. I looked across at Angela Blackwood and to my astonishment she grinned at me. Her whole face lighting up. The expression was gone in an instant, so I could not be entirely sure the smile had been aimed at me, but no one else seemed to have remarked it. It then dawned on me that perhaps Miss Blackwood was a lot more clever than I had given her credit. None of us knew for certain whether or not she could speak to Maisie, though I strongly doubted it, but I felt certain that the killer sitting waiting for the long day to pass would find the impending séance extremely uncomfortable. In fact they might find it so unnerving that their behaviour might give them away. Who knew what a woman desperate enough to kill in a cell full of sleeping women might do if she thought there was a chance she was shortly to be unmasked? I looked across once more at Miss Blackwood. She nodded very slightly at me. I felt a slight shiver down my spine. I had no doubt she knew exactly what I was thinking.

CHAPTER
EIGHTEEN

A most unexpected visitor

Once matters had been decided an uneasy calm settled in the cell. I determined to watch the other women closely as the day wore on. However, watching others when you are closely confined, as I quickly discovered, is no easy task. Not least because the others were openly watching each other. All of us were also exhibiting a natural nervousness, not unlike that of a group of hens who fear a fox is in their midst. Abigail Stokes had withdrawn as far from the group as she could. Her eyes darted back and forth as she surveyed the group. Martha Lake had also retreated to a corner and was staring dismally at the small barred window high above us. Her thoughts were obviously elsewhere. The twins were seated once more on the bench. Jasmine leant against her sister with her eyes closed and snored softly. Eunice's bright eyes met mine and I sensed she had appointed herself guard to her sleeping sister. Angela had taken a third corner. She appeared awake and watchful. She flashed me another broad grin when my eyes encountered hers. This left only Constance, Mary, and myself. There remained one corner, but all three of us seemed to be inhibited by politeness from retreating.

We had been too slow to claim our space and now sat uneasily in the middle of the cell. "It is surprisingly comfortable sitting on the floor," said Constance.

"A relaxing of the rigorous nature of deportment from time to time is certainly welcome," answered Mary.

"Indeed," said Constance lowering her voice, "I own that I have not given up corsetry entirely as some of our Sisterhood have done, but I have — shall we say — expanded my standards."

Mary and I dutifully gave a small chuckle each. Though I liked both women well enough[1], internally I was well aware of a rising boredom. It seemed likely to me that unless one of us broke under the strain the day would be spent in conversation on undergarments, knitting, and other such inane mundanities. Soon I might be the one resorting to murder. Certainly none of the women here were currently exhibiting either the political fanaticism or hysteria that the newspapers claimed was the norm for the "Shrieking Sisterhood".

I became dimly aware that Constance and Mary had moved on to discussing the merits of stockings of various materials. "I prefer woollen," injected Jasmine, startling us all. "So cosy."

"I thought you were asleep, dear," said Eunice.

---

[1] Though not well enough to acquit them of murder without further investigation! What a strange life I have led.

"Resting my eyes, dear," returned Jasmine. "As if one could sleep when one is so hungry."

It struck me that it must be well past breakfast time. However, having been overfed by Fitzroy, who seemed to have an affection for childish, stodgy puddings, much like Bertram did, my stomach had issued no complaint.

"It does not seem a good idea to summon the guard," said Mary sadly.

"Talk of food may provoke them," echoed Constance.

"I do feel a little faint," moaned Jasmine.

"You have missed one meal," snapped Angela. "There are many in this city who daily count themselves lucky to have even one crust of bread."

"I don't want bread," said Jasmine, "but I rather fancy a coddled egg."

"Good luck with that," said Abigail under her breath.

"It's not a blooming hotel," countered Angela.

"I would ask you not to speak to my sister in such terms," said Eunice, sitting very upright. I wondered if things were about to start up again, but not in the way I wanted. I strongly doubted that fighting over foodstuffs and stockings would bring us any nearer to exposing the murderess. This was all becoming extremely wearisome. So it was with both alarm and relief that I jumped at the sound of my name being called in a male voice. The guard, who had told me to call him "Mark", stood at the bars.

"Miss St John," he said coldly, "you are wanted." I struggled to my feet.[1] Mary put out her arm to support me. I thanked her and made my way across to the door. Mark opened it and ushered me out.

However, instead of taking me along the corridor towards the room Fitzroy favoured, he took me in the direction of the visiting room. When he opened the door I strode in expecting to see Richenda or perhaps Bertram. However, the person seated at the table was the very last person I expected to see.

"Good morning, Hans," I said, my voice a little shaky. I put up my hand to push the pins further into my hair. "I am afraid we have not been provided with basic facilities. I must look quite atrocious."

Ever the gentleman, Hans rose and took my hand in his. He led me to the seat, which he pulled out for me. "You never look anything other than enchanting, Euphemia."

I collapsed into the hard seat. "Hans, I am so very sorry."

"Whatever for?" he asked sitting opposite me.

"You must be furious," I said. "And rightly so."

"I am," said Hans with sudden frown, "but not with you. Richenda had no business involving you in her madness. Good God, a public march! What could she have been thinking?" He gave me a slight smile. "I acquit you of all involvement, Euphemia. I know you

---

[1] It is not easy for a lady in skirts to rise from the floor with any degree of dignity, especially when she is unused to such an exercise.

131

are far too well-bred to ever have considered making such a public spectacle of yourself."

My mind flashed briefly back to the moment I had pulled that policeman from his horse. "It is not that I do not support the Sisterhood, Hans. Richenda may well have believed I would be happy to attend." I found myself defending my employer with some warmth.

Hans made a passing gesture with his hands. "Be that as it may. The genteel support of the cause through letter-writing and the occasional well-regulated meeting for ladies of class is one thing. What Richenda has done is quite another."

"You support the cause?" I asked, suddenly curious, but Hans, as ever, was diplomatic. "I do not oppose it *per se*. I am unsure if the majority of women wish for the vote and to take on the extra burden of interesting themselves in the matter of running the country. I believe that many of your sex, Euphemia, are far too busy, and indeed successful, in running their own homes and families. It seems to be that the role of a woman supporting a man is a very full one. Or should be." His face darkened.

"I believe Richenda is motivated by belief rather than any desire to cause trouble for . . . anyone . . . " I trailed off. There was a rigid set to Hans's mouth.

"I do not suppose you would be able to tell me where my wife is?"

"She is not at the hotel?"

"I arrived this morning to be told she had left me a note. She obviously was well aware that despite her request not to follow her to town, I would do so.

Despite the fact I have told her I am engaged in the most serious business at present. Not to mention that she has left Amy alone for far too long. It was her decision to adopt the child, and I was happy to acquiesce to her request, but my wife must be brought to realise the consequences of her actions and that she cannot flit from one frivolous scheme to another as she did before our marriage."

I quailed inwardly. It was out of character for Hans to criticise Richenda in front of me, or anyone. He must be extremely angry. "What did the note say?" I asked gently, praying she had not mentioned anything about investigating the incident at the railway station.

"It merely said that she had an errand to do and that she would return shortly, if I cared to wait."

"Then she knew you were coming to town?"

"I think that after your incarceration she rather expected it," said Hans dryly. "No, tell me, Euphemia what is this all about?"

"It started with the deaths you have doubtless read about in the newspapers, but since then one of my cellmates was strangled in the night and we are all under suspicion."

"Good God!" exclaimed Hans. "I am sorry for my language, but to think my wife has placed you in this position. It is unconscionable."

I reached out a hand and laid it briefly and lightly on his arm. "Hans, I really do not blame anyone. Or if I do it is the authorities for the way they handled the march. They rode in amongst us on horses."

Hans paled. "I read of it in the newspapers. I have already written to my MP." He sighed. "For all the good that will do."

"At least it isn't Richard," I said with a smile.[1]

Hans gave a short laugh. "No that would be a pointless exercise." Then he straightened his cuffs and gave me a level look. "I assume you believe the girl who was killed witnessed an action that one of your other cellmates perpetrated during the march? And that this is most likely connected to the firebombing?"

"It could be something else, but that does stretch incredulity."

"Of course, she could have been killed for any number of reasons, but this does seem the most likely. From what I gather, Wilks was a high-ranking civil servant without immediate family. From the limited information I can gather he appears to have lived beyond what I would have expected of even one in such a position as his. Of course, he may have been a beneficiary of a legacy we do not know of."

"But you think he may have been committing embezzlement?"

Hans looked shocked. "Euphemia, as a banker I would never say such a thing about someone without absolute proof."

"But his manner of living arouses your suspicions?"

---

[1] I was referring to his brother-in-law Richard Stapleford, Richenda's twin, who was currently a Member of Parliament, which demonstrates beyond doubt that civic standards have fallen to an all-time low.

"That I will allow. He also went to one of the very best schools, so as well as his position in the civil service I am certain he had connections of significance."

"So I've heard," I murmured.

"Of the people he knew well I have come across five names that he appears to be most closely associated with: Sir Henry Bassington, a peer in the House of Lords, who he fagged for at school; Mr Humphrey Wellington, a man who shocked his family by making a fortune in trade — stockings and other ladies' fripperies, I believe; Mr Eric Bellows, a man of independent means who spends his time hiding from his wife and five children in the better clubs in town; Sir Harrington Blake, a stalwart of the Foreign Office; and lastly Mr Pierce Clegwood, a merchant banker."

I had been listening with astonishment, but at the last name I collected myself, and closed my mouth that had fallen open in a most unladylike manner. "I assume it is the last man to whom we owe a debt for this information?"

Hans shook his head. "I have helped him make sound investments. There is no debt."[1]

"I am very grateful you have gone to such lengths, Hans, but what do you expect me to do with this information?"

"I have been aware that you and Bertram have certain connections . . . " He let his words hang in the air for a moment, then continued, "I believe that they

_____
[1] Sometimes he could be absurdly literal.

will find these links too, but I think I have found them quicker. I hope it might help."

"I don't know what to say," I said.

"It is the least I can do, not merely because of what my wife has done, but because of what I must do." A feeling of unease crept over me. After all his assurances, was Hans about to evict me from his home and my position?

CHAPTER
NINETEEN

Anyway...

"I am afraid I must distance my family from this situation. My position at this time, being of German heritage, is not a comfortable one. I cannot afford to draw unwanted attention to myself. I am only a director. I can always be voted out of my position, and there is the estate to think of. It is not yet self-sufficient and a great many people's livelihoods are in my hands."

Tears pricked at the back of my eyes, but I swallowed hard and said in as strong voice as I could. "I quite understand."

"You are truly a most estimable woman," said Hans.

"Let us hope another employer will think so," I said with a quivering smile.

Hans frowned. "What? No! Good heavens, as if I would . . . how could you . . . " He took a deep breath. "I meant that I must remove both Richenda and myself from London for the present. You will, of course, return to us as soon as you are released. To that end I have engaged Sir Bartholomew Farnsworth. I understand him to be one of the country's best defence lawyers, if not the best."

"Heavens, Hans," I cried, "I cannot allow you such expense."

Hans raised one of my hands to his lips and said, "You are worth it, my dear. Now, I must leave you, and I feel a dashed cad for doing so, but it is in the certain belief that Sir Bartholomew will have you home very shortly." And he left the room.

"Drat," I said aloud to the empty cell. I could just imagine what Fitzroy would make of me suddenly having obtained the services of highly regarded legal counsel. As soon as Mark appeared to return me to my cell, I told him of what had passed. "I fear Fitzroy won't like this," I finished lamely.

"Not like? He'll go bloody ballistic," said Mark and then blushed. "Sorry," he said. "This place isn't conducive to gentlemanly behaviour."

"I find it odd that at one moment you gentlemen treat me like some kind of fragile flower and the next you throw me in a cell with a murderess." I knew my tone was not conciliatory, but I was growing weary of having my loyalties tugged in all directions. It was at that moment that the dreadful sergeant appeared.

"Give 'er to me. She's wanted."

Mark and I involuntarily exchanged looks. "Ah, so that's how it is," said the horrible little man. "A little tit for tat. That's what you were up to. Never mind. I'll hand her back to you when I'm finished."

"I am under orders to return her to her cell," said Mark, barely masking his confusion.

"Yeah, well, there's another toff what wants to see her. Dead popular, she is. Free with your favours, are you, luv? I can be a lot nicer than I appear."

I shrank back against Mark. "I'll take her down," said Mark firmly.

"Suit yourself," said the sergeant. "Same room."

Mark led me off. I glanced back and the sergeant blew a kiss at me. "You've got to get me out of here," I hissed at Mark. "I do not feel safe with that man on duty."

"I'll see what I can do," said Mark in my ear, as she showed me into the room. There, waiting for me, pacing backwards and forwards, was an agitated Richenda. She flew at me the moment Mark let me go and embraced me. I managed to brace myself against the wall. "Thank goodness, you are safe."

"Has Hans seen you?" I asked.

"I saw him coming out of the station as I was heading in. I hid behind a dustcart. It was terribly smelly, but I needed something of decent size to ensure I was not spotted. Rather reminded one of playing Hide and Seek with Bertram when we were all little. Little rotters that we were, Bertram had a habit of climbing into cupboards to hide and we always locked him in! But as to Hans, I rather think he has come to take me home."

A mulish look crossed Richenda's face, so I said, "I think you should go. Amy will be missing you."

Richenda pursed her lips and gave herself a little shake.[1] "I have every intention of going home," she said. "I do not need to be fetched like some lost

---

[1] Not unlike her horse, which she unfortunately resembles, does at home when it is refused an apple.

puppy!" She stretched out a hand to me and touched my arm. "I am very sorry to be leaving you, but you are right that my daughter needs me and at least Bertram is now in town. You, at least, seem to find him of use."

"Yes, he has visited me."

"I only came to tell you what I had discovered before I left." A mischievous smile crossed her face, "I must say, if this what all your adventures are like they must be jolly fun." I looked at her aghast. Richenda batted her hand in front of her face as if she was waving away a fly. "I do not mean the being locked in jail part. That was frightful." She gave an exaggerated shudder and I had a sudden vision of her regaling her next suffragettes meeting of all her doubtless exaggerated sufferings, and glowing in their praise.

". . . is rather fun!"

"What did you say?" I asked. "I am afraid I am rather tired."

"I said this business of asking questions and looking for clues is rather fun."

"What have you done?" I enquired, trembling inwardly.

"No more than you asked," replied Richenda. "I asked around a few of the ladies I know — and it took quite some doing, I can tell you. If she had been of my class it would have been easier, but I had to ask a whole range of people to get down to that level."

I looked at her blankly.

"The woman, who died, Agnes whatever her name was, lived in a reasonably respectable boarding house."

140

I straightened up at this. So she had not lived in the store as was the norm for shop girls.

"She was on reasonable terms with other women on her floor. Their landlady is a bit of a dragon, but I soon saw to her! Tried to pose as a lady come down in the world. As if! Anyway, she insists they all take dinner together at night. She locks her doors at 9.30p.m. to prevent immoral behaviour. As if immoral behaviour is confined to the hours of darkness. Although I suppose some of it is."

I bit my tongue and let her ramble on. I hoped she would soon reach the point.

"Anyway, one of the dead girl's particular friends was a Miss Annie Hallows, who is also a suffragette."

"So that's how you traced her!"

Richenda gave me a fearsome look and continued. "Of course, the landlady is much against such matters, so it had created a bond between them. So much so that Miss Hallows told me she and Agnes had been planning on attending the march together. I take it from other comments she made that Agnes was not of an overly likeable character, but she was a most devout suffragette." Richenda gave a big sigh. "Anyway," she reiterated, "the morning of the march Agnes received a letter."

"What did it say?"

"Miss Hallows only knew of it as she heard the landlady knocking early on Agnes' door. She admits to opening the door a crack. Apparently, it was most unusual for the landlady to venture above stairs unless she was collecting overdue rent and Miss Hallows says

Agnes what's-her-name was always very correct and proper about paying on time. Anyway," — under the table I clenched my right hand into a fist, allowing the nails to dig in a little — "anyway, she was very put out. The landlady, that is. She said she had been awoken early by a special post for Agnes what's-her-name and she was not used to such goings-on in her lodgings."

"How did Aggie react?"

"That's the funny thing. Miss Hallows said she seemed quite as put out as the landlady. She certainly hadn't been expecting anything. She said as much and the landlady immediately said she hoped it was not bad news. Miss Hallows said she — the landlady — is a bit of a nosy parker and it was clear Agnes what's-her-name wasn't going to get rid of her now until she'd opened the letter. I mean, I would have told her where to get off, but I suppose if you owe the roof over your head to someone else, you can't be quite as forthright."

I gave a level look, but Richenda missed my meaning entirely.

"Anyway, so here is Miss Hallows still listening through the crack in the door and she hears Agnes . . . "

"Her name was Aggie Phelps," I said, unable to contain myself any longer. "Are you sure you got the right woman?"

"No, you're right, that was it. Agnes. Aggie. Probably short for Agnes anyway. Anyway, Aggie said it was a letter from a friend, but Miss Hallows said she sounded very surprised. Like she had looked at the signature and given a little start."

"That's a bit fanciful," I said gently.

"Anyway," continued Richenda, "the landlady was not one to easily give up and she pressed hard for more details."

I held my breath.

"But all Agnes — Aggie — said was, and her Miss Hallows is quite clear on this because of what came afterwards, that a good friend required an urgent favour and would Mrs Breem, that's the landlady, excuse her at once." Richenda sat back in her seat, looking pleased.

"What do you think of that?"

"What happened afterwards," I prompted.

"Oh yes, that. She — Aggie — knocked on Miss Hallows' door and explained she would no longer be able to go with Miss Hallows to the march. Miss Hallows said you could have knocked her down with a feather. They had been arranging it for months. Apparently women who work only get so much free time, so it had been quite a big issue for them to arrange time for both of them to be off work together. So much so that Miss Hallows said she became quite angry. Something she regrets now, of course, and demanded to know the reason why there plans were to be so disrupted, but all Aggie would say was exactly what she had told Mrs Breem and no more."

"Did she say if Aggie seemed frightened?"

"I thought of that," said Richenda triumphantly. "Miss Hallows said she did not seem frightened. If anything she seemed more confused. As if she was very much taken aback by what was in the letter. Miss

Hallows pressed her for details, but Aggie said the letter swore her to secrecy and she could not on her honour as a suffragette say more. Indeed Miss Hallows said it took a great deal of persuasion even to get her to say as much. Of course, now she believes the letter was instructing Aggie to take the firebomb to the station and she blames herself for not insisting on knowing more."

"Does she think Aggie was capable of such a thing?"

"I asked that too," said Richenda beaming. "Poor thing broke down at that. I had to make her a cup of tea on her own little stove. Not that she drank it."

I kept silent. I could only imagine what tea made by a woman who had never set foot in a kitchen might be like.

"She said if anyone had said anything like this about Aggie before the incident she would have refused to accept it."

"Yet now that it has happened she is not so sure?"

"Exactly. I must say, you are quite sharp, aren't you, Euphemia? Anyway, the poor woman was all torn up about it. It seems Aggie was certainly one for smashing windows, something her friend had never done. Miss Hallows is not your more militant type, if I am any judge. Much more your reasoning female. I get the impression that perhaps Aggie was trying to make her more active. She said that Aggie had invited her to some meetings which were not generally open to the public, but she had had to decline due to her work commitments. She said she was very glad she had not gone, as goodness knows where it might have led her. I thought it rather a shame as it might have led us to some women who knew more. I'm presuming they were active planning meetings for civil disobedience."

"I should imagine so," I said. "Honestly, Richenda, you have done brilliantly. Where was this lodging?"

She gave me the address and then leant over the table, speaking in a quiet voice. "I think that means one of the women in the cell with you must have been in on it too. What about the dead girl?"

"You mean another member of the group feared she might say give them away?"

"Exactly," said Richenda," and killed her to keep her own skin safe. I imagine after you have killed once it gets easier. Like eating oysters. They seems so slimy at first, but one quite gets into the way of it after the first half-dozen."

"I can't imagine Maisie involved in any such thing. She was so timid."

"Maybe she saw or overheard something? That would be enough if you feared being hanged, wouldn't it?"

"I suppose so," I said slowly. "I hate to think these murders are down to the Sisterhood."

"I agree," said Richenda, looking downcast. Then she collected herself. "Anyway," she said, "I must go back to the hotel and Hans."

CHAPTER
TWENTY

A séance in a cell

By the time I returned to the cell the day was ending. A dusky light filtered through the bars, casting a grey shade over the faces of the women inside.

"Ah, you're back," said Angela. "I reckon we can start now."

"Start what?"

"Why, the séance, of course."

"What was it this time?" asked Abigail Stokes with a sneer. "Swapping recipes with the sergeant?"

I could not repress a shudder at the thought of Sergeant Givens. "No, it was my employer."

"Been fired, have you?"

"No, he has hired a lawyer to defend me."

"Blimey," said Abigail, looking genuinely taken aback. She turned her back on me, but I thought I heard her mutter, "that'll set the cat among the pigeons."

It occurred to me then that perhaps giving the impression I might be out of there soon might put me in danger. I mentally shrugged off the idea. After all, I had seen nothing on the day of the march and hopefully whoever was Aggie Phelps' partner-in-crime knew that. I found myself reconsidering the women in the cell in the light of what Richenda and I had discussed. It seemed most likely Abigail Stokes would be the culprit. Although I could not rule out Angela Blackwood, but she was an odd fish and I could not rightly pin down her motivations.

"In a circle, please, ladies," said my odd fish.

"Oh, Eunice, do you think we should?" wavered Jasmine. "I doubt Father would approve."

"Then if Miss Blackwood really can contact the dead perhaps he will come through and tell us so," said the practical Eunice.

Miss Blackwood flashed Eunice a smile. "Who knows what spirits are liable to come this way? I have no control over the dead. I can only petition that they speak to us."

Mary Hill settled herself on the floor, arranging her skirts neatly around her. "I am quite content to join the experiment, Angela," she said, "but I have to tell you I am not a believer." I sat down next to her.

Abigail sighed and said obscurely, "In for a penny" and joined us. The Pettigrews were fussing, sweeping aside space on the floor for themselves to sit.

"So unladylike," muttered Jasmine. "Our dresses will be quite ruined."

"Sister, I hate to tell you," said Eunice, "but when we are released we will need to burn these clothes. I fear mine are already infested."

"Aw, Gawd," said Abigail, "I should have bleedin' known it! Fleas."

"It was really only a matter of time," said Mary Hill. "This place is most insanitary."

Martha Lake stood hesitating on the edge of the circle. Angela looked up at her. "I need everyone if this is to work. Do you have a moral objection, Mrs Lake?"

"No, not as such," said Martha. "I too wonder if it right to tamper with such things, but I am aware it is not unusual for séances to be held in the best drawing rooms."

Abigail gave a crack of laughter at this. "Let's hope the spirits don't mind coming down a bit in the world."

"They are beyond such things," said Angela haughtily. "Now, if you would take your seat, Mrs Lake. I can begin. I warn you that this is not a light undertaking and there are dangers —"

"Oh dear," wailed Jasmine.

"But," said Angela, raising her voice to speak over her, "if you follow my instructions no harm will come to anyone in this room."

The rest of us looked up expectantly at Martha. She sat down in the space left between Angela and Eunice. "Now, if you could all hold hands," said Angela. "It is not quite as dark as I would like . . . " Even as she said it the light level dropped and the air turned a little colder. "Ah," said Angela, "good. If you wish you may close your eyes. Especially if it helps you concentrate. Once we begin at no time must the circle be broken. Hands are only to be released when the spirits had been banished once more."

"So you do send them away?" asked Jasmine.

"Yes," said Angela.

148

"But I thought you said they were always with us," commented Mary. She said this in an enquiring sort of tone rather than a sarcastic one, but Angela's eyes flashed.

"They are indeed always with us, Miss Hill, but it is only with the help of a medium that they can transcend into a communicative state. It is from that state I will banish them when we have concluded our business."

"Oh, that sounds so unpleasant," said Jasmine. "To be wandering the earth, seeing all, but being able to speak to no one."

"That is why people such I as exist," said Angela, her tone becoming increasingly acerbic. "Now, let us begin. I will call upon the spirit of Maisie and ask her to come to us."

"So you do not have a spirit guide," asked Martha. "I thought that was quite the fashion."

"I do not need one," snapped Angela. "I am in harmony with the other side."

"How uncomfortable," muttered someone.

"Ladies! Please! We are here to avenge the death of a poor young girl. Let us take this situation seriously. Unless, one of you has good reason not to wish tonight's séance to work?"

"Like being the murderess?" said Abigail Stokes. "I'm game. Call 'em up."

The other women all nodded. The coldness of the cell was increasing. I told myself that this was only because we were seated, and not moving around as we were wont to do to keep warm. "I warn you my voice may change," said Angela, "but do not be afraid. Others may speak through me."

Jasmine suppressed a little squeak as a glance from Angela quelled her. "Now to begin with, if you could all close your eyes and concentrate on the face of Maisie." I closed my eyes and lowered my head so I could peek, hopefully unseen. Angela's eyes were open and she raised her head to the ceiling. Why, I wondered, do mediums always look at ceilings. If we were outside under the sky it would make sense, but inside surely the spirits would not be hiding among the ceiling plaster.

"Is there anybody there?" she said in a deeper voice than she was wont to use. "I am calling to the other side as my grandmother and mother did before me. I am Angela Blackwood and I am using my gift to open the channel between worlds. Is there anybody there, who wants to speak to anybody here?"

There was silence. I felt a shiver run down my back, but I was more concerned it might be a flea than a spirit. My left leg was beginning to ache. None of us gently bred ladies were used to sitting on the floor. I straightened my shoulders and adjusted my posture to a more correct attitude. As I did so I could have sworn I felt a light touch on the nape of my neck. My head shot up. My eyes open, ready to spot the trickery. Everyone in the circle was still present. Indeed with the exception of Angela, whose eyes appeared to have rolled back in her head, everyone else had their eyes tightly closed.

"OMMMM!" said Angela in a deep voice. "OMMMM!"

I observed Jasmine Pettigrew screw her eyes even tighter shut, so her face resembled nothing less than a pickled walnut. Abigail Stokes heaved a large sigh. Mary's face was calm. Martha had her head bowed like mine. Was she too sneaking a glance around the circle? She looked more as if she was at prayer.

"I feel you," moaned Angela. "I feel you! Someone is coming through." Jasmine gave another little smothered squeak of dismay. Honestly, her lips were almost touching her eyebrows now. She looked grotesque. Could this be a sign of guilty fear or simply superstition? I would have expected a schoolmistress to have a cooler head,

"Here she comes," wailed Angela in a high-pitched screech that made me wince. Though I remained rather colder than before, I did not believe this was caused by any wandering spirits. To me Angela's theatrics were almost comical. I had no doubt she was a fraud. Why on earth was she doing this?

And then it dawned on me, as bright and clear as when the sun breaks through the clouds, that the only way Fitzroy would have allowed me to stay in a cell with a murderess would be if he already had someone on the inside. Someone, who like me, was attempting to stir things up and get a response from the killer. A woman who also realised our time here was limited. I might appreciate Hans's attempts to get me out, but I did not want the potential shadow of a crime hanging over me for the rest of my life. If no murderess was caught then people would always wonder.

Angela had to be Fitzroy's plant! I decided to give her a little moral support.

"Ohhh," I said softly, "does anyone else feel the temperature dropping? I have the most dire sense of foreboding." Mary Hill opened one eye and gave me a quizzical look. I added a shiver in for extra conviction. I lowered my voice. "I'm serious. Something is happened." Mary gave a little shrug and closed her eyes. In the background Angela continued her low moans. "M-m-m-Maisie," she was now calling. A real shiver did go down my spine as I recalled finding the poor girl's dead body, lying cold and twisted on the cell floor. It had been dawn and at the time I had not been able to see her clearly, but now my imagination was filling in the missing details, her eyes pale as cornflowers staring sightlessly, the pinched aspect of her pretty face that told of so many missed meals, but above all I remembered how she had looked little more than a child. Richenda's adopted daughter came from lowly stock, if her life had taken a different turn, she could so easily have ended up like Maisie, poor, over worked, and scared. In my mind's eye little Amy aged and became Maisie. I had felt despair and pity when Maisie died, but now I felt fury.

And then for no reason at all I heard myself say, "I never take sugar with China tea."

CHAPTER
TWENTY-ONE

A noose is offered

"So do you know who did it?" Fitzroy's voice snapped like a whip.

Fitzroy had summoned me only moments after the séance ended, which was just as well as my comment had not gone down well with my cellmates.

A moment after the words had left my mouth, Martha Lake had broken the circle and stood up. "If no one is going to take this seriously, I do not see why I should stay sitting on this filthy floor," she had said. With the circle broken, Angela had thrown herself to the floor and writhed a bit. I had been impressed by the performance; Eunice even more so.

"Look what you have done!" she'd exclaimed at me, rather than Martha who had actually broken the circle. "She told you how dangerous it was for someone to interrupt her when she was in a trance."

"I don't recall —" I began.

"Totally thoughtless," echoed the usually passive Jasmine, then looking at Mary. "What do you think we should do for the poor woman?"

"You're not going to tell me you believe any of this nonsense, are you?" said Martha, who was now seated on the bench.

"I think, as we do not know exactly what is happening," said Mary calmly, "that we leave Miss Blackwood alone unless she looks to be in danger of harming herself."

"But she may be beset by spirits!" said Eunice, who appeared to have embraced the situation most fully.

"Nah," said Abigail. "It's all an act, isn't it? Bet she was hoping one of us would own up."

"Do you think so?" asked Mary. "An interesting plan if not a successful one."

"But why should she do such a thing?" whispered Jasmine.

"'Cause like the rest of us she wants out of this bleedin' place," said Abigail.

At this moment Mark, followed by another two policemen bearing the evening bowls of slop, had arrived to escort me to see Fitzroy once more. The first thing I noticed on entering Fitzroy's office was that there was no sign of food. My stomach growled loudly.

"So do you know who did it?"

I opened my mouth to respond, but Fitzroy held up his hand. "Be careful what you say," he added. "Time has run out and whoever you name I shall more than likely put a noose around their neck. This business needs to be ended."

I closed my mouth.

154

Fitzroy's face darkened. "Come on, Euphemia, don't go squeamish on me now. You always knew where this was leading."

"I am uncomfortable about the idea that someone might meet their end on my word," I said. "Doesn't there need to be evidence?"

"That can be sorted," said Fitzroy dismissively.

I tried to feel surprise, but failed. I was all too familiar with Fitzroy's methods. "I spotted your person — your woman," I said stalling for time.

"I would have been disappointed if you hadn't. Now, stop stalling and tell me who you believe did this?"

"Wilks or Maisie?"

"Are they different?" Fitzroy's voice carried a note of surprise rarely heard from the spy.

"I don't know," I said honestly. "For all I know they could have all conspired together."

Fitzroy sighed. "Kill the lot and let God sort them out?" He saw my shocked face. "It's a quote, Euphemia. Not what I am intending to do."

"Why the sudden urgency?"

"Your admirer, Muller. He got you the best lawyer in London. There is no way I can keep you under lock and key without charging you, so I am forced to let you all go on bail. Though whether the others have the material wealth to post bail I have no idea."

"I am sorry," I said contritely, "but I could hardly tell him what was really going on, could I?"

Fitzroy rubbed his hand over his face. "No, I suppose not, but this has left me in a bad position. I am needed abroad. The Balkans have broken out. I fear Wilks's death will need to go unanswered."

A silence hung between us.

"I could continue to look into this," I said eventually.

"I could not possibly ask you to do this. Even if poor little Maisie was killed on your watch."

"I have already agreed," I said.

"Hmm."

"I have discovered where Aggie lived. Not at the store but in a boarding house and that she received an unexpected letter on the morning of the march that made her change her plans."

"Who on earth told you that?"

"Richenda. She did a little detective work on her own before her husband removed her from town."

"Richenda, what a surprise," said the spy. "I take it you still did not tell her about me?"

"Of course not," I said wearily. "It was her idea to investigate. She comments she had observed me doing this previously and that it looked rather jolly."

"Well, she has certainly done better than you. Perhaps I should have left her in the cell."

"I did try to provoke a fight," I said. "Abigail almost stabbed me."

"I doubt that," said Fitzroy shortly. "What did Bertram unearth? I assume you had him on the trail as well?"

"That I have yet to learn, but Hans did tell me the name of Wilks's closest friends."

"Did he indeed? And why did he do that?"

156

I ignored his comment and related the names. "I've heard of Blake, of course," said the spy, "but nothing that would suggest he might be involved. I will pass the other names on to Edward, but I do not hold out much hope. Such men, even if involved, will ensure they have got good alibis. Still, we can put a watch on them for future activity. We live in interesting times." He gave a swift smile and then said sharply, "Why do you think Hans did this for you?"

"He said he had become aware that I had certain connections."

"And what did you say?"

"Nothing," I responded. "I thought it would be dangerous for both of us — Hans and I — for me to do so."

"Hans is proving to be somewhat dangerous himself," muttered Fitzroy. He paced away from me. "The stockings," he said suddenly. "We were a pair short. One of the pairs was also of distinctly superior quality. Several were torn and stretched, but this may have been caused during the protest."

"March," I corrected.

Fitzroy waved my comment aside. "I do not like to leave untidy ends. I am half minded to choose one of your companions at random if you will not give me a name."

"That would be crossing a line, even for you," I responded sharply.

Fitzroy turned and walked up to me. Right up to me. He came so close it felt uncomfortable, but I would no more have stepped back than I would have turned my back on a tiger. "You have no idea of what lines I am prepared to cross," he said coldly, "when the necessity arises."

"Let me try and find the solution," I said, aware I was now practically begging to do a task only a few minutes earlier I would have done a great deal to avoid.

"I shall have to leave in three days, no longer. I will release you and your cellmates on bail. I will ensure all of them are free, and you shall have your time to choose one. Or I shall pick one for you."

"I need more information," I said quickly. "Addresses and the like."

Fitzroy indicated a file on his desk. "You can take that. You will be going straight to the bail hearing and not back to the cell."

"You had it ready for me!"

"Of course," said the spy, and called for me to be taken before the judge.

CHAPTER
TWENTY-TWO

My modesty is once again endangered

The luxury of bathing is much underrated. I lay deep in a hot bath in the hotel where Richenda and I had been staying. As I had hoped, Hans had kept the suite on. Though when I turned up in a hackney cab in my dishevelled state it was rather touch and go as to whether they would let be back into the hotel at all. Fortunately, I had summoned the image of my mother at her haughtiest to mind and treated the reception staff with such contempt they doubtless thought I was a duchess travelling incognito. Or perhaps even minor royalty, I mused, dipping my head under the water and moving my head from side to side so my long locks flowed like a mermaid.[1]

I sat up smoothing my hair, heavy with water, from my face. I could almost imagine those nights in the cell had been nothing but a bad dream. Then I heard the door of the suite open.

---

[1] A habit I had begun to enjoy since joining the Muller estate. My mother had frowned heavily on indulgent bathing. She felt it weakened one's moral fortitude.

My heart, usually a most reliable organ, jumped into my mouth. It is only the maid, I told myself, but I was already looking around for whatever in a hotel bathroom might be used as a weapon.[1] My fingers reached for the bath plug. My modesty warred with my desire not to be drowned in my own bathwater. I heard footsteps outside the door.

"Euphemia?" called a familiar voice.

"Oh, good heavens, Bertram. I am bathing!"

Then came the strangled sound of a gentleman in an unconscionable position. It was as if Bertram had swallowed his tongue and his neck tie all at once. After this came a gargling noise and that distinctive cough the well-educated male gives to show that he has realised he has committed a fatal breach of etiquette and is about to pretend it has not happened. "I will await you in the coffee room downstairs," he said in uneven tones. Then I heard the sound of footsteps fleeing.

Every maidenly bone in my body should have been shocked, but I could not help it. Laughter bubbled inside me and within moments I was laughing so hard tears were streaming down my face. After the horrors of the cell, to be back in a position where one had to consider niceties once more struck me as both delightful and ridiculous.[2]

---

[1] The answer, in case you were wondering, is not very much. Unless you are particularly lethal with a sponge.

[2] My mother would never consider being caught in the bath a nicety of social etiquette, but in my defence she has never had to urinate in a bucket.

160

Eventually when I felt I was edging close to hysteria, I did something my mother would have approved of and stuck my head under the cold water tap. The sudden sensation of coolness sobered me. I dried myself and dressed, but then came a real problem — one gentlemen do not have to consider. My long hair was still very wet and would take some time in front of the fire to dry. There was no way I could venture downstairs with wet hair. Even I would not go that far! I rang for a maid to light the fire and also to convey a message for Bertram to attend me. I described him as my brother, a ruse we had used to effect before, and ordered that coffee be brought up for us both. I also added a small brandy to the order for Bertram. From the sound of him earlier, he would need it if he were to face me.

Bertram was, after all, a man and would have been unable to resist imagining me in the bath. He would doubtless be acutely aware that when he saw me again the image he had been imagining was still present, though now under clothing. I suppose it is a measure of those I have associated with of late that I even entertained such thoughts.

Bertram and the coffee arrived together. The maid placed the tray on a little table and gave a little bob before retreating. Bertram opened his mouth to speak, but nothing happened. I passed him the brandy. He downed it in one and gave a little splutter. "Ah, thank you, Euphemia."

"I have told the staff we are brother and sister," I said. "I hope you have not done anything to counter this idea. This is, after all, a suite and the two bedrooms are separated by our private saloon."

"Good God! I can't stay here!"

"Indeed," I countered passing him a cup and saucer, "then I assume I will have to find Wilks and Maisie's killer alone. I had rather hoped you were going to help me. Fitzroy gave me this." I passed him the list of names and addresses the spy had given me. "Only one is missing. A Martha Lake. I assume she is at this moment being followed and we will receive the information in due course."

Bertram, now forced to hold his cup and saucer and the document, admitted defeat and sat down. "Have we been officially, unofficially, asked to do this?" he asked in a defeated voice.

I avoided the question. "Surely you wish to see justice done?"

I passed him another page that I had written on the hotel stationery. "These are the names that Hans managed to find of men who are associated with Wilks. Below that is the boarding house where the dead suffragette in the railway carriage was resident. Richenda managed to discover that she received a letter on the morning of the attack that changed all her plans."

"Never tell me the Mullers are working for Fitzroy!" exclaimed Bertram.

I shook my head and poured myself a coffee. "No, they were doing their best to aid me." I gave him a level look.

Bertram flushed slightly. "Of course I won't let you down," said Bertram. "I realise the killer must be caught for your name to be cleared."

"Which is why we need to go to the Gilded Lily. Have you heard of such a place, Bertram?"

The question was redundant. I could see from the puce colour that had suffused his face he knew exactly what the Gilded Lily was. "Bertram," I said in a reproving tone.

"Clubs. Men talk in clubs," replied Bertram in a strangled voice. Then he resorted to bluster. "What the devil does Fitzroy mean telling you about such places?"

"This whole affair started with the firebombing and as no one seems to have witnessed anything, we must begin with the victims. Wilks was a known frequenter of this place."

"But damn it, Euphemia, such places don't go about giving information out. They are used for their discretion."

"Which is why while you are unsuccessfully talking to the owners of the establishment, I will be talking to the girls."

CHAPTER
TWENTY-THREE

The Gilded Lily

The Gilded Lily was an unassuming terraced townhouse. Bertram was still virtually straining at the leash. I had got him here by the simple expedient of telling him that if necessary I would go alone. I did not share with him that Fitzroy, fearing exactly this, had not divulged the address.

"Damn it, Euphemia! I'm not going in there!" said Bertram after he had paid off our cab at a discreet distance from the club. "I should never have let you talk me into this."

"Well, then I shall have to go in alone."

"You are hardly one of their normal clients," said Bertram with a sharpness that was uncharacteristic.

"I shall pose as a girl looking for work."

At the point, Bertram caught me by the arm, and held it uncomfortably tightly. "You cannot, you absolutely cannot, do that," he said.

I looked him direct in the eyes. "Why not? When you first met me you thought I was exactly what the girls inside are."[1]

---

[1] This was a little unfair. See our first encounter in my journal *A Death in the Family*.

Bertram flushed so darkly I would have feared for his heart if his grip on my arm was not so bruising. "Your association with Fitzroy is damaging you."

"How dare you! I do not *associate* with Fitzroy," I exclaimed hotly. "You are hurting my arm."

Bertram let go at once. He looked more shaken than I had ever seen him in all our adventures together. "This is not right, Euphemia. Neither of us should have to enter this place."

"I think I will find that being threatened execution by foreign spies is far worse."

"It is not the same thing at all," said Bertram. "Here, your virtue may be in jeopardy."

"I assure you I am quite capable of looking after myself. I will be in no danger," I countered in what I hoped was a more reasonable tone. Though, I admit, if Fitzroy had shown me the manoeuvres he had promised, with which he claimed I would be more able to protect myself, I would have felt more self-assured. Still, to date I had found my quick wits[1] and loud scream had stood me in good stead.

"Euphemia, you have no idea what such a place is like."

"It can't be worse than the farm I grew up on!"

The look on Bertram's face should have been immortalised in oil. Really, men, gentlemen in particular, seem to need to believe that ladies should know nothing about reproduction, which when you consider we do the actual producing is quite ridiculous!

---

[1] This may sound immodest, but . . . well, yes, it is immodest.

I used Bertram's momentary shock to escape and head down the steps to the side door. I assumed that those I wished to talk to would definitely be using the tradesman's entrance. I knocked smartly on the door. I had a last glimpse of Bertram's shiny brogues pacing back and forth in indecision before my attention was taken by the door opening.

In truth I had prepared many speeches to achieve my objective and been happy with none. My intention had been to discuss matters further with Bertram until he showed his intractable side. As it was my heart was in my mouth as the blue door opened. I had a moment of panic, but managed to suppress my impulse to flee simply because I couldn't bear to see the smug look on Bertram's face if I bottled it.

"Good evening," I began before the door was even fully open. "I . . . "

An older man with greying hair, who was clearly a butler but dressed with exceptional style, said, "Lizzy?" in a pleasant baritone. "You are a little late."

I opened my mouth and closed it again.

"You are Lizzy, aren't you?"

I managed to nod my head. The man gave me an avuncular smile, "Well, my dear, this is a good, clean house and you will be well looked after. You have no need to worry. Come in."

Dumbly, I followed him inside and along a narrow passageway. "I'll take you in and you can meet some of the other girls. I'm sure they will take to you. From what I can see you are quite different from the others and we do like to offer our gentlemen variety."

166

My faint hope that Lizzy might have been the new kitchen maid faded. "Now, what you're wearing is quite nice, but the master has laid out your costume for the evening in one of our downstairs rooms. It is not so very different from what you are wearing, but it is, shall we say, more accessible." He opened a door to a large kitchen. A not unpleasant smell of cooking wafted out. "I suggest you get yourself a decent dinner," continued the man, "and maybe a glass of wine for courage." He ushered me in. As I passed him he gave me a little pat on the bottom. With difficulty I managed to suppress both my small squeak and my immediate response to turn round and slap him.

The scene in the kitchen, if it hadn't been for the apparel the occupants were wearing, would have been quite domestic. Several women were seated around a kitchen table. Three were finishing their dinner. All of them looked to be no more than nineteen. One of them, the youngest at around seventeen, was licking her knife with an expression of ecstasy. "That were right lovely, Mother," she said to an older woman, who was tending to pots on the range. "I don't rightly remember when I had such a good plate."

"Just as well," said one of the other three, "Father's said how we've got a busy night." There was an outburst of giggling. None of the them seemed to have noticed me yet or perhaps they were simply not interested. The diners, and another woman, who was mending a stocking, were all wearing the lowest-cut bodices I had ever seen. Moreover they were loosely laced, doubtless to expose the ladies' assets to full

167

effect. The woman darning had her feet up on another chair and her skirts pulled up around her thighs, so that a glimpse of lacy underwear could be seen. I must have been staring for one of the diners suddenly said, "Cover your purse up, Gladys! You're shocking the new girl."

"If she's shocked by what I've got wait till she sees what Sir Toby's got!" said the darner. The others burst out laughing.

"Oh, come on," said the first girl. "We were all new once." She got up and came over to me. "I'm Betsy, but the gentlemen call me Lucia. They like nicer names. Most of them." She guided me to the table. "Mother, can you get the new girl a plate?" she called over to the cook. "She's not actually our mother," she said in a low voice to me, "but she likes us to call her that. Rather like Father. He's the butler. You watch out for him. He's all nice and friendly, but a couple of tots of gin and he's got more arms than an octopus. Probably tell you how he gets it on the house as he works here. Don't you believe it. We don't service none but the proper gents."

A plate of stew was set in front of me with a cup of tea. "Get that down yer, love," said the cook. "Father said how the master wants you to get straight to it. He always reckons it's best with you new ones to throw you right in."

"Oh, are you doing the fainting virgin too?" asked the seventeen-year-old. "Only that's kind of my thing."

"Ah, but you, Janie, are a blonde and this girl has got lovely chestnut curls." She fingered my curls and I fought an impulse to pull away. "Quite a different look. So there's no need to be getting your claws out."

I still hadn't spoken. I now understood that Bertram had been completely and utterly right. This was a stupid plan. None of these women were going to open up to me easily and I had no desire to chat with an octopus. At the moment Bertram could have been as smug as he liked if only he would walk through the kitchen door and rescue me right now. I looked over hopefully, but the door stayed resolutely shut.

Mother followed my gaze. "There's no point thinking of leaving, my dear," she said firmly. "The master has paid good money to your family for you and until you work it off you'll be staying here. If you had any doubts you should have left them on the doorstep. Gladys, keep an eye on her, we don't want a bolter." She turned back to me. "Not that you'll get far. Father keeps the house locked up tight. Now, when you've finished, Gladys will take you through and show you your get-up. Nice red one, it is."

I managed to swallow a few mouthfuls of stew and tepid tea. My mind was racing frantically. I decided to play the foolish, scared girl, which was not too far from the truth. Hopefully, if I was quiet and seemingly compliant, I would be able to grab a chance to escape before the evening's entertainment began. The doors might be locked, but did they lock the windows too? There had to be emergency measures in case of fire, didn't there?

It was with a sinking heart I followed the girl through to another little room. Laid out on a chair was a ghastly, indecent scarlet gown. "I'll leave you to it," said the girl. "If you've trouble with the laces I'm sure Father will be only too glad to help." She gave a little chuckle as she closed the door behind her. I heard the sound of a key in a lock. I immediately ran over to see if the key had been left in the lock, but luck was not with me. The room was small with only the chair, a mirror, and a small barred window. I felt an absurd impulse to burst into tears. I gave myself a little shake and mentally told myself that if I could face death in a pigsty, I could certainly get myself out of an ordinary house. I struggled into the dress and redid my hair, ensuring I tucked some long and pointed pins securely into my locks for use in extremis. I took a look in the long glass mirror and saw a woman I sincerely hoped my mother would not recognise.

The dress did not have sleeves, so I was unable to slide a pin up my cuff. When the door opened once more, without a single knock, Father stood there. He looked me up and down in both an intimate and a professional manner. "Very nice," he said. "Now, I don't want to be indiscreet," he gave a faint laugh, "I'll leave that to your first caller. A very nice gentleman, if I might say so. The master is starting you off with the gentle ones, who don't have particular interests. Now, I need to ask you, have you got your sponge in? Do you need any help? I can send Mother in if you do?"

By now I was barely following what he was saying. "I always ask the new girls after what happened to little Annie. Before you were born, that was, but the poor lass died giving birth. Blamed myself for that one, I did.

Not that we don't get the odd by-blow here, but if you're in trouble Mother is very good with dealing with things if you speak to her early enough."

"What happened to the baby?" I said. My voice sounded faint and far away.

"Oh, she had a particular and he took it. Paid for it to be raised nice by all accounts. Most of the clients wouldn't have been interested, but he was quite young himself, and sweet on Annie, if I'm any judge. Some of them do get that way, you know, but it's only the real nobs that ever marry one of you girls. Got to be someone who can spit in the eye of the world, and him, well, he were a clerk or some such. Though how he found the money to visit her as regular as he did, I'll never know. Anyway, you got your sponge in like a good girl? Not foolproof, of course, but you give yourself a good wash out when he's gone and more than likely you'll be as right as houses."

I couldn't say a word. If I opened my mouth I was certain I would be sick. "Right, follow me, girl," said Father. He led me down a maze of twisting passageways, up a small flight of servants' stairs, and opened the door to a bedroom with a huge, over-decorated four-poster bed. "Washstand and water by the window," he said. "Gent will have a key."

Then he locked me in. I ran to the window, but it was barred. I looked around the room for a weapon. Nothing which seemed better to me that the pins in my hair. I had no idea if I could hit a man hard enough with a chair to incapacitate him. I thought briefly of explaining my position, but I had a sinking feeling that

I would not be taken seriously. In fact, my caller might even believe it was part of an act. No, the only way out would be to bloody the unsuspecting gentleman and flee screaming. If I was lucky, the real Lizzy was at this minute knocking at the door.

I pulled out the largest, sharpest pin from my hair, and stood with my hands behind my back.

It was not very long at all before I heard the sound of a key in a lock. My gentleman caller had arrived. I stepped to one side of the doorway and tensed, ready to strike. I hoped he was a small man and not some large, "beefy" individual.

With terrible slowness the doorknob turned . . .

CHAPTER
TWENTY-FOUR

My gentleman caller takes me by surprise

I raised my hand ready to strike. If I could pierce the back of his neck and leave the pin in then he would be too occupied with twisting and extracting it rather than pursuing my flight. Luck was with me; the man emerging slowly the door was not tall. I lunged.

With a speed that caught me completely off guard the man span and caught my arm. He twisted it painfully and then released me immediately.

"Euphemia!" cried Bertram. "What the hell are you wearing?"

"Bertram, what on earth are you doing in a prostitute's room?"

"I could damn well ask you the same!"

Unaccountably tears pricked my eyes. "I expected you to talk to the men downstairs," I said. "I never dreamed you'd . . . "

Bertram finally closed the door behind him and pushed me back into the room. "For your information," he said coldly, "my intention was only to talk to the girl. I would have paid her well for her time, but not availed myself of her . . . usual services. Not that that is any of your concern." He looked me up and down. "What, may I ask, were *your* intentions?"

"I was going to stick you in the neck with this pin and make a run for it," I said and burst into tears. "Oh, Bertram, you were right. This place is awful. It was a stupid idea."

Bertram's face softened at once. "Might I suggest that next time you intend to take someone by surprise, you do not yell at the same time as you intend to strike?"

"Did I?"

"You said something along the lines of 'take that, you vile . . .' I caught your arm at that moment, so I do not know how you intended to finish your statement."

I could not look him in the face. "Beast," I said quietly. He put one hand on my shoulder and with the other raised my chin up, looking deep into my eyes.

"Did anything happen?" he asked intently. "You can tell me. I won't judge you."

My tears stopped at once. "No," I responded, shocked. "I am not that foolish, nor that helpless." I brushed a hand over my eyes. The top of my bodice slid slightly and Bertram retracted his hand as if he had been burnt. A slight smile quivered at the edge of my mouth. "I do not believe it will be possible for us to retrieve my clothing. I fear I must ask you for your coat once we are outside."

"But how the devil do I get you out?" asked Bertram.

"You escort me to the door like a gentleman. For all I know the women here actually do that with their clients. It is only once we reach the doorstep that we both take to our heels. I do not believe this establishment would wish to draw attention to itself through a chase outside."

"My reputation will be in tatters," said Bertram mournfully.

"*Your* reputation?"

"No one would recognise you like that. You look the image of a lady of the night."

As there was nothing I could say to this outrageous comment, I did the next best thing and inveigled Bertram into the tightening of my laces. "I can't possibly," he said blushing.

"Do you want this dress to fall off me as we flee?" I enquired. "Because that is exactly what will happen if you don't! The laces tighten at the back, there is nothing for you to see."

"I fear I have already seen far too much," muttered Bertram as he began to tug away.

"At least you did not walk in on me in my bath," I could not resist adding. I immediately regretted this as Bertram tugged so tightly I thought my lungs would leap out of my chest. When I was finally as respectably adjusted as was possible, we sat down on the edge of the bed together to wait.

"I will let you work out the timing," I said.

Bertram raised an eyebrow quizzically.

"I have no idea how long such things take," I snapped. "If you were a pig or a bull . . . "

"Quite. Quite. I think this about long enough."

"Really?" I asked in genuine surprise.

"The men who come here do not expect lengthy trysts," said Bertram to the carpet.

"It hardly seems worth their while to come at all," I said.

Bertram made an inarticulate strangled noise and rose. He held out his arm to me. I sighed and stepped up into character, draping myself over his arm in an overly affectionate manner. Then he opened the door. "Deep breath," he said, but whether he was referring to keeping up my corset or my courage I could not tell.

He led me out and along the corridor in the opposite direction from the servants' stairs. I had already discounted those. I knew Father had locked the back door. The corridor opened out onto a plush landing, filled with aspidistras and flouncy curtains that were quite out of the mode, but I assume they held appeal for the older gentleman I could see milling around in the lobby below.

The stairs led straight down into a large lobby that was also used as a welcoming area. Cushioned chaise longues abounded and small tables with drinks decanters and cigars were dotted around. So were the girls I had seen in the kitchen earlier. My quick view allowed me to see at least seven gentlemen in suits had arrived for an evening's entertainment, and given the number of girls I had seen here they no doubt had to wait their turn. One man caught my eye. "Isn't that . . .?" I whispered to Bertram.

"Good Gad, so it is! At least *he* won't mention he's seen us here."

We made our way gradually to the main door. A liveried man opened the door for Bertram. He released me from his arm and we made as if to give a fond farewell. My lips brushed Bertram's cheek. At that moment I saw over his shoulder Father emerging into the room with a fresh tray of drinks. "Run," I yelped and we, as they say in common parlance, legged it.

"Did you really have to yell in my ear?" asked Bertram when we were safely back at the hotel. We had stopped on a street corner for me to assume his jacket and I had walked past the hotel reception with my nose so high in the air that I had almost fallen over my own feet, but it had worked. We were now back in the safety of our suite. I had changed into respectable attire and Bertram had ordered a pot of tea. He was sitting close to the fire, although the evening had remained mild, and was rubbing peevishly at his ear.

"I have explained that I thought we were about to be caught," I said. "I am sorry your ear still pains you. I am sure you will recover shortly." I poured him a cup of tea. "Have a biscuit. These ones have jam inside them."[1] Bertram's eyes lit up and he took two biscuits. I forbore saying a word. Although I had noticed of late that his neck had started to bulge over his collar. No one could call Bertram overweight, but with his enforced sedentary lifestyle — due to a heart condition from his childhood — as he grew older he needed to

---

[1] In many ways men remain at heart boys.

watch what he ate. I made a mental note to speak to him about this at a more convivial time.

"At least Rory is still in the country," I said.

Bertram showed the whites of his eyes for a moment like a startled horse. "For God's sake, Euphemia, never mention any of this escapade to him! He'd gut me like a poacher's rabbit!"

"He is your servant."

"Yes, well, someone should explain that to him," said Bertram grumpily.

"His employment is at your disposal," I said candidly.

"I know," said Bertram reaching for a third biscuit. Really, if he went for a fourth I would have to say something now. "But he is damn good at his job — and not just his. He drives the motor better than I do now."

"That would not be hard," I murmured under my breath.

"He helps my factor, talks to my tenants, and I honestly don't think the cook could manage half as well if he wasn't keeping his eyes on the accounts."

"He sounds indispensable."

"He is," agreed Bertram gloomily. "It's not that I don't like the chap, but we've been put off terms of such familiarity when we've being off doing stuff for King and Country that the distinction of rank is at risk of being lost."[1]

I sighed. Bertram mistook my meaning.

---

[1] Bertram had no idea I was an Earl's granddaughter and thus far above him on the social scale.

"Oh no, I didn't mean . . . " said Bertram, "I mean, you're more like one of the family. It's an entirely different case. If only the man wasn't so damn fond of you. Makes this a trifle awkward."

"Seeing as he jilted me, I do not think you have cause for concern."

"Did he? I always thought it had to be the other way round?" asked Bertram looking very surprised. "Odd fellow."

I felt the blush rush into my face. "Anyway, now we are safe and recovered we must discuss what we will do next."

"I am not going back to that place," said Bertram mulishly.

"Neither am I. I assume your comment about seeing Mr . . . " Bertram held up his hand in alarm. "About seeing a senior public figure there," I amended, "means you think that any gossip about our escapade will be curtailed?"

"God, I hope so," said Bertram fervently.

"Good, then we have no reason for our killer to believe we are on their tail."

"I suppose so," said Bertram warily. "What are you thinking?"

I gave him my most innocent smile. "Why, simply that we invite some people for tea."

CHAPTER
TWENTY-FIVE

I send out polite invitations

Using Fitzroy's list I had sent invitations to the Pettigrew sisters, Angela Blackwood, Mary Hill, Constance Woodley, and Abigail Stokes to come to tea at the hotel prior to my departure to the countryside. Martha Lake was not invited as no one had yet discovered who she really was. I gave the ladies twenty-four hours' warning. It would have been polite to wait longer, but I was afraid the killer might leave the city. Declining my invitation so shortly after our incarceration would throw up further suspicions. Bertram disagreed with me. The next day, after I sent off the notices, we sat together in our suit arguing agreeably over a private lunch.

"You have told me you looked into the names that Hans gave me and nothing particular struck you," I said.

"I had a few chats around the clubs," admitted Bertram. "It seems Wilks and Blake were together at Oxford. Firm friends and all that. No falling out that I can hear of. The banker chap is, well, a banker chap."

"Like your brother?"

"Half-brother," said Bertram, "but I see your point. To be honest, if anything I imagine Hans will have warned anyone off gossiping with his asking around. I mean, he might think his chap is going to keep it to himself, but a German asking around about you at this time? No one is going to keep that quiet."

"He's half-German."

"He might only have German toes," said Bertram, "but it would be enough to raise attention. I know he belongs to a few of the clubs, but he's noticed more than most. Not that I don't think he is a decent fellow and all that, but . . . "

"He may have done more harm than good with his questioning?"

"I am afraid so."

"Then that is exactly why we need to get my cellmates gathered together. I do not discount that one or any of the men Hans named may have been involved in these murders, but we know without a shadow of a doubt that one of these women murdered Maisie and that is our way forward."

"Unless it was that nasty sergeant you told me about."

"Don't," I said holding up my hand. "That would make things far too complicated. If the police are involved . . . "

"Corrupt policemen trying to make the suffragettes look guilty?" suggested Bertram.

"That has to be a flight of fancy too far," I said.

Bertram shrugged. "We have been involved in stranger things. Spies and pigs. That will be all I shall say on the matter."

"If we get all the ladies together," I explained, "we can stir things up a bit and see if we get a response. I have a number of suspicions and this is a perfect way to voice them. No lady will abandon afternoon tea mid-pot."

"From what you have told me, Euphemia, they are hardly all ladies."

"With the exception of Abigail Stokes, who does indeed strike me as the rougher type, I believe the others will conform to the hotel's standards."

"What about Martha Lake?"

"I never seriously considered her. Undoubtedly a gently bred woman well into her middle years. I have no doubt that Fitzroy was right and that she was merely attempting to protect her husband by not disclosing her real name."

"Yes, well, I suppose the more ladylike the person the less likely they are to be prone to see violence as a solution," agreed Bertram. "Remind me of the possible motives for each of these women, as you see them."

I ran through each of the women in turn. "Hmm," said Bertram. "It's all a bit weak, and bringing in that stuff the chap told you at the brothel is really stretching it."

"Do you not think it possible Wilks may have had an illegitimate child?"

"Of course it's possible. We know he wasn't a backgammon player."

"What have games got to do with anything?"

Bertram gave a little cough. "Forget I said anything. I am agreeing with you. It's possible, but even if it were so why should she murder him now?"

"Well, someone must have had a reason," I said waspishly. "We know Aggie Phelps was no one of any account."

Bertram raised his eyebrows at me. "Fitzroy said she might have been involved in the more militant side of the Sisterhood. Wilks might have been in the wrong place at the wrong time."

"And Aggie Phelps might have been too careless?"

"Exactly," said Bertram. "So much of this may be coincidence."

I wanted to deny it, but in my heart of hearts I knew he had a point. "Where we stand is this was either a suffragette attack that went wrong or it was someone out to murder Wilks and blame it on the suffragettes."

"Kind of thing Fitzroy would do," said Bertram.

"No," I said. "He wouldn't do that. He believes in the cause."

"I think you romanticise the fellow," said Bertram sharply. "He is not a gentleman."

I laughed out loud. "Gentleman is certainly not the first word I would use to describe him," I said, "but I believe him to have the best interests of King and Country at heart."

"Hmm," said Bertram and speared a potato with unnecessary force. "I do not think you know the half of it."

"Probably not," I agreed equitably. "But I also do not think Fitzroy would have made such a song and dance about investigating this affair if he or his people had had anything to do with this. In fact," I said, tilting my head on one side to consider the matter properly, "I do believe he would have arranged matters much more neatly had he wanted Wilks dead."

"Good grief, Euphemia! Such things should never enter a lady's head. She should have no knowledge . . . "

"I am hardly of the norm," I countered.

"No," said Bertram with feeling, "though I agree if Fitzroy was investigating this and using you, he did not know the killer and wanted to know as soon as possible. He was even prepared to endanger you to get at the truth, if you will remember!"

I let this pass. "Other than inviting the women to a private tea," I said. "I cannot think of what to do next."

"No, I suppose not. There does not appear to be anything else to investigate."

"Let's hope that their reaction to the hotel's delicious biscuits puts them off their guard," I said.

Bertram sighed and reached for another portion of peas.

The ladies arrived promptly the next day and were shown into a private room that Bertram had hired. None of them had declined my invitation, which had disappointed me slightly. I realised as I wrote my introductions that I had completely missed out Constance Woodley from my musings. Was it through some nefarious skill that she had left so little an impression on me? I introduced Bertram to them all as my cousin and chaperon. It had been either this or my fiancé, and I really had no desire to be engaged again.[1]

The Pettigrew sisters wore enormous hats with rather tattered dead birds on them. They both chirped away rather like their deceased headwear once must have. The hotel was "so lovely". "Father would have approved so much." "Bertram St John" was "so handsome". Bertram did not correct him on his name, but he pulled a face at me behind their backs. I shrugged apologetically. I should have thought of that. Angela Blackwood made magnificent inroads on the cake and Mary Hill showed her breeding with every sip of tea. Constance chattered about her children. Abigail Stokes had barely spoken since she had arrived, but now we were beyond the bread and butter stage, and the little repast was in full flow, she suddenly piped up, "So who do you think did it, Euphemia?"

Eunice and Jasmine twittered in distress. Angela Blackwood choked on a piece of cake had to be slapped on the back, before she gave way to hearty laughter. Mary, I noticed, paled slightly. "You mean who do I think killed Maisie?" I asked directly.

"Why else would you invite us all here?" responded Abigail. "You know as well as the rest know — or should know," she added glancing over at the Pettigrew sisters, "that until this murderer is found that we shall all be under suspicion for the rest of our lives."

"What an unpleasant thought," said Mary softly.

---

[1] Besides, it might have given Bertram ideas.

"Oh, I don't know," said Angela, "a bit of rumour and gossip can add spice to a character."

"We are firmly against spice," said Eunice.

"Indeed," said Jasmine, "Father would never have any in the house. He said it inflamed passions." Her voice sank to an almost inaudible level at the end of her sentence.

"It would not surprise me if it was the horrible sergeant," said Eunice.

"You may not know, ladies, but when we handed in our stockings in they were one too few in number," I said opening the topic carefully.

"No mystery there," said Angela. "Can't abide the things. I like the free flow of air around my nether regions." At this remarkable announcement both Jasmine and Bertram looked close to fainting.

"Well, that suggests it could not have been you. Unless you managed to stuff the stockings somewhere else," said Abigail.

"The cell was too small for anything to be hidden, in my opinion," said Mary.

"I have my reasons for believing Angela innocent," I said grandly.

"What were those, dear?" asked Eunice.

"I am afraid I am not at liberty to say," I responded, "but I am afraid a small deception was practiced on you. Angela and I are on the same side. That is all I can say."

"What?" said Angela. "You're a . . . " Whatever she was going to say was rudely cut off by Abigail.

186

"Why you flaming idiot!" she exploded. "I was the one looking out for you! That's why I had the shank. I'm F's woman!"

And with this outburst she destroyed my carefully reasoned argument to Bertram as to why, of all them, the militant Abigail Stokes was most likely to be the killer.

CHAPTER
TWENTY-SIX

Logic is applied

Bertram gaped at me. "Is that true?" he mouthed at me. I did not know what to say. By calling herself "F's woman", Abigail had proved to me that she knew about Fitzroy.

"Not sure what you are talking about," Angela said, "but if the looks you've been giving your cousin are anything to go by I don't think we are in the same hockey team, as it were."

Before I could ask what games had to do with it, Bertram interrupted. "No, she is not. However, as you were not wearing stockings, madam, and Miss Hill is convinced there was nowhere to conceal them, it would appear that you cannot be the murderer."

"Have you given any thought to motive?" asked Abigail sarcastically.

"Of course," I responded. "The woman who died with Wilks . . . "

"Wait a minute . . . you are assuming this is all connected with the firebombing?" said Angela.

"But it has to be," I said startled.

"Why?"

"Because Maisie was scared. She knew something and she was afraid of admitting it."

"She told you this?" asked Abigail.

"More or less," I hedged.

"Could it not have been that she recognised someone in the cell and thought they were likely to kill her?"

"That would be true whether or not Wilks was involved," said Mary. "The logical question to ask is that if she thought she was in danger of her life, why did she not tell the police?"

"They were not very nice," said Jasmine. "Could she have been as afraid of them too? We had children at school, didn't we, Eunice, who were afraid because we were teachers and they had heard all teachers beat children."

"You mean in the same way that all policemen beat suffragettes?" asked Abigail.

"Or perhaps she simply thought that no one had seen her witness whatever she saw," said Mary.

"You mean she did not want to get herself in any deeper?" asked Bertram.

"Unfortunately that does make sense," said Abigail, whom I could not help but notice was far better spoken now she had revealed her true allegiances. "She would worry the police might think she was involved."

"But if she was innocent," said Bertram.

Abigail gave him a scathing look. "She was a young girl of no family and no position. I doubt whether her innocence would have mattered much. They would have wanted her information and also suspected her."

"Was she wily enough to know that?" I asked.

"I think you will find that someone who has had a hard life learns to be very cautious," said Abigail. "If she thought she could get away with it then she would have kept her silence."

"But whatever do we think she had seen?"

"If this line of reasoning is sound," said Mary, "and that is far from clear, the only thing that makes sense is that she saw something of the firebombing of the carriage that killed two people."

"Did anyone know Aggie Phelps?" I asked.

"I did," said Abigail. "She was being watched. She'd been involved in vandalising a telephone exchange. No one was sure how far she would go."

"So she could have set the bomb herself and accidentally been immolated?" asked Mary.

Jasmine gave a little moan and Eunice produced a lavender-scented handkerchief to dab at her sister's brow. "This is not at all the friendly meeting I thought we were coming to," she said with a hideous regard for grammar.

"If that were the case," Abigail answered, ignoring Eunice, "why would Maisie have been scared by what she had seen? And Euphemia is right. The girl was terrified. I tried to talk to her, but she was almost out of her wits with fear."

"None this makes any sense," said Mary. "No one knows why Aggie was in a First Class carriage and it is likely now that they never will."

"I know," I said. As one the ladies turned towards me. "She received a letter on the morning of the march and changed her long-arranged plans at the last minute. Someone asked her to go."

"At last we get somewhere," said Abigail. "Who sent the letter?"

"I don't know," I admitted.

"So you do not have it?"

"No, but I have two witnesses who can testify to its existence."

"I suppose that's something," conceded Abigail.

"But why send her there?" piped up Bertram. I could tell by the look on his face he was feeling a little left out.

"The only logical assumption is she was there to ensure Mr Wilks did not leave the carriage," said Mary.

"Oh my heavens," said Eunice, quicker on the uptake than I had imagined. "Does that mean she knew she was going to die?"

"A suicide mission?" asked Abigail, frowning.

"What if she was simply told that for the sake of the March she needed to keep Wilks away?"

"That would be such an evil thing to do," said Jasmine faintly.

"Murderers are not generally known for being pleasant," said Angela. "It goes with the occupation."

"Are you seriously suggesting," said Mary, "that one of us sent Aggie Phelps to her death simply to kill Wilks? Why Wilks?"

"That is the question, isn't it?" I answered. "There are many possible motives. I have managed to track down Wilks's closest associates. They range from bankers to civil servants to men in high ranking public service."

"Public school," said Angela. "Oxford too?"

"Yes," I said.

"So this has nothing to do with the Sisterhood," asked Eunice.

"Except to use it as a scapegoat," said Angela bitterly.

"And Aggie, who we already know was prepared to work with the more militant side probably felt she was being given a secret and special assignment," I said.

"Which is why she did not question the letter. Nor tell anyone," said Bertram. "She thought it was a test of her loyalty."

"When in reality she was being used by someone unscrupulous," said Eunice.

"And someone who was in contact with the Sisterhood. Someone who knew how to put out feelers to a would-be militant, one who would obey without question."

"How terrible," said Jasmine. "To think that a fellow sister would be able to do such a thing."

"Except we have no more proof of this than we do that she was not killed by the over-zealous Sergeant Givens," said Mary. "We may be attempting to use logic, but we are building castles in the air. Everything we have outlined is based on assumption and not fact."

"It is however a fact that you are the illegitimate daughter of a senior personage, isn't it?" I asked Mary.

Mary flushed. "I do not believe that my heritage has any bearing on this issue," said Mary shaken.

"Unless Wilks was your father," said Abigail.

"Or knew who your father was, and was about to expose him," I added.

"Interesting idea," Abigail acknowledged.

"That you could think me capable of such a crime is an insult beyond bearing," said Mary rising from the table. "Whatever you think of me, I could not possibly have set the firebomb or whatever it is they do. Ask her." She nodded at Angela. To me she said, "And to think I thought we might be friends."

Angela shrugged. "We were side by side in the March all the way."

"Why on earth didn't you say anything?" asked Abigail.

"No one asked me," said Angela. "Besides, I have a rule never to answer to any man."

The sound of a door slamming signified Mary had left us. I looked at Abigail. We both looked at the Pettigrew sisters. Angela began to laugh. Constance shifted uncomfortably in her seat but continued to hold her peace.

CHAPTER
TWENTY-SEVEN

I accuse...

"That certainly narrows down your options," said Abigail. "Perhaps it was a two-person job? That would make more sense." She gave the Pettigrew sisters a hard look.

"Us?" gasped Eunice and Jasmine in uncanny unison.

"It is no more likely than Angela and Mary working together," said Abigail.

"Except these two have known each other all their lives and we have no evidence that Angela and Mary were even friends," I answered.

"True," said Abigail.

"But why would we harm a soul?" asked Eunice.

"Perhaps if we looked into the demise of your father's business we would discover that Wilks or one of his associates had something to do with its failure?" suggested Bertram.

"I am afraid Father suffered from both poor health and poor judgement," said Eunice.

"Eunice, you must not say such things about our sainted Papa," said Jasmine.

"The man was a fool," said Eunice. "Face it, Jasmine, it was our work that kept the family afloat and denied us the chance to spend our lives as we might have wished."

"Oh, no!"

"Would you not have loved to have had children?" said Eunice. I saw tears well up in her sister's eyes. "Father's foolishness and selfishness denied us the lives we should have lived." She turned to the rest of us. "That is why I am so in favour of female emancipation. No woman should have her life dictated to her by a man — especially a foolish one."

Jasmine accepted Bertram's handkerchief and began to weep uncontrollably. Bertram bravely patted her hand.

"If Wilks had been our father," said Eunice angrily, "we might have had cause to kill him, but sadly it was not until Father's death that the reality of the situation came home to me."

"Oh, you mean when Mr Walker died so unexpectedly?" said Jasmine, reaching out a hand to her sister. "I am so sorry."

"Who the hell is Mr Walker?" snapped Abigail.

"He was the suitor Father forbade me to marry. Shortly after Father's death he applied to me again for my hand in marriage. I accepted him and the next day he was run down by a horse and cart. He died with my name on his lips."

I felt a terrible impulse to laugh. Her story sounded so melodramatic, but then I saw the very real pain on each of the sisters' faces and I knew they were telling the truth.

"I do notice that none of you have suggested I had anything to do with it," said Constance suddenly. "For which I am very grateful. Yet, if it would help clear the air, I am willing to swear on the Bible that I did not kill Maisie, nor have I any connection to Mr Wilks's death. I am sure the hotel staff could obtain a Bible if we were to ring for one."

Bertram looked at me. I shrugged. "I am sure that will not be necessary, Mrs Woodley," he said gently. "You have not figured in our investigations in any way."

"But we did!" said Eunice angrily.

"I think we should leave, sister," said Jasmine.

"It has been a most interesting tea party," said Angela, rising from her chair. "But I think we have come to a natural end. It appears to have been established that none of us present could have killed Wilks and by extension none of us had any reason to kill Maisie. Thank you for an entertaining afternoon, Miss St John, but I do believe I have had my fill." And will that she left the room. Eunice and Jasmine hugged each other, wept on each other's shoulders, and then gathered their possessions and also left the room. Eunice cast me one final look of sheer loathing.

"If I might go?" asked Constance. "I would like to be home before the children go to sleep." Bertram held the door open for her.

Abigail Stokes sat back in her seat and picked up her teacup. "That was a spectacular mess," she said.

"At least we established none of the women present were guilty," said Bertram.

"Do you not believe women are capable of deception, Mr Stapleford?" asked Abigail.

"She's one of Fitzroy's," I said. "I thought it was Angela."

Bertram, who had started at the sound of his real name, said in astonished accents, "He uses women?"

"What precisely do you think I am, Bertram," I snapped. "A camel?"[1]

"But . . . but . . . but," said Bertram.

"But she is an amateur," said Abigail. "Whereas I am the real thing, and as such I will shortly be leaving the country on the King's work. It must therefore fall to you to finish the case. I hope Fitzroy's trust in you was not misplaced. I cannot say I have yet seen anything that inspires my confidence."

"All the avenues are closed," said Bertram.

"Not all," said Abigail. "I must go. I have a boat to catch."

As the door closed behind her, Bertram said, "I suppose this means Martha Lake is our murderer, but even Fitzroy could not discover who she was."

"Perhaps it was Givens," I said thoughtfully. "At least I know what we need to do next."

Bertram eyed me with alarm.

"We have overlooked something, Bertram. We must go to the boarding house and retrieve the letter sent to

---

[1] This was a particularly sore point, as I had promised myself I could go and see a real camel at the Zoological Gardens while in town with Richenda. It now seemed very unlikely this would happen.

Aggie Phelps. I doubt it will be signed, but it will be somewhere to start."

The better part of the day had passed, and besides both Bertram and I were mentally exhausted. Bertram went for a smoke and a drink in the bar, and as the day was fair and mild, I decided to go for a short stroll. I left Bertram a note in the suite. I felt certain if I told him he would attempt to stop me, but in this genteel part of the metropolis I felt it was unlikely I would come to harm. I also had a strong desire for a new pair of gloves. It had not escaped my attention either that I was missing now not one but two outfits.[1] There would certainly not be time for a fitting, but perhaps I might get some ideas of the latest fashions on show and describe them to the Mullers' seamstress.

It was with such innocent schemes in mind that I set foot outside the hotel. I wandered down a few streets, taking care not to stray too far away. I purchased some delightful lilac gloves, took good note of the finery on display, and was about to return to the hotel when disaster struck.

---

[1] The suffragette one bought by Richenda, which I would never wear again, and the one I had discarded at the Gilded Lily.

CHAPTER
TWENTY-EIGHT

I am exposed (again)

I could not hide nor pretend I had not seen her. My mother sat in the window of a respectable coffee shop and glared at me. Then she raised one imperious finger and beckoned. I entered the coffee shop in a state of extreme shock. I was unclear whether it was the sight of my mother sitting by a window (on public display!) or whether it was the sight of my mother at all that shocked me most. The last I had heard she was still living in the country, tending her subdued livestock and tyrannising the local population with piano lessons.

"Is something wrong with little Joe?" I exclaimed as I reached her table.

"Good afternoon, Euphemia. Yes, I am quite well thank you. Allow me to present my dear friend Lady Blake. We were in the Primrose League together. Celia, this is my daughter, Euphemia Martins, whom I certainly raised to behave in a much better style than this."

Words failed me as I turned to offer my hand to Lady Blake. I recognised her at once. Her eyes met mine and she gave a tiny, almost imperceptible shake of her head. "Charmed to meet you, Euphemia," said

Lady Blake. "I can assure you your little brother is quite well. I understand he is staying with your mother's local squire and learning how to shoot."

I could only surmise that she had never met Joe, she gave out the potentially lethal information in such a casual manner. "He will be fine, Euphemia," interrupted my mother. "He is only to be allowed to shoot rabbits and squirrels."

My brother is a lovely boy of infinite charm, which he needs as he frequently gets himself into mischief. I knew my brother would never deliberately harm anyone or any livestock, but I also knew he was not very good at listening or obeying instructions. It seemed the height of folly to place a lethal weapon in his hands.

"Are you in town long?" enquired my mother. "Would you care to join us for a cup of tea or would you prefer to stand there looking like a waitress?"

"I am so sorry, Mama," I said contritely. "I have recently had a great deal on my mind. I believe I will shortly be leaving London to return to the Mullers' estate, but I am uncertain as to the date of my departure."

"And as to whether it is significantly far in the future to allow you to consume a cup of tea?" asked my mother.

A waiter appeared behind me and set a chair. I sat down automatically. "I do not wish to intrude," I said, casting a worried look in Lady Blake's direction.

"Very well," said my mother, as soon as I was seated, "I can see you are eager to be about your concerns. I will be writing to you shortly about a matter of import."

"I see," I said numbly.

"Indeed, it is very good news," said Lady Blake. "Your mother and I are shortly to become related. Or have I said too much?"

"My daughter has yet to meet your cousin, the Bishop. She has been living in the country for some time with friends."

"Bishop?" I asked, confused. I was ignored.

"But there is nowhere like one's home, is there?" said Lady Blake.

"Are you going to work for a Bishop, Mother?" I asked. She gave me a hard stare.

"Don't be ridiculous, Euphemia. People of our station do not work. I am going to marry him."

"I am so delighted for you, my dearest. It seems both our fortunes are on the turn," said Lady Blake.

I rose, mumbling my excuses, and left. I wandered back to the hotel in a daze. Bertram met me in the lobby. "Ah, good, I was beginning to think about dinner," he said. "Shall we dine in the restaurant tonight?"

"No, I need to speak to you in private," I said.

Bertram cocked an eyebrow. "Have you been out solving things without me? I thought you were only going to buy gloves. How much trouble can you get into buying gloves?" His voice rose slightly. "I should have known. Something dire has happened, hasn't it?"

Indeed," I said, "I met my mother and she told Martha Lake exactly who I really am."

With this parting shot I headed towards the lift. There was an audible pause behind me. Then I heard

Bertram positively hoofing it towards me. In the lift cage his face was a veritable picture, as he struggling not to demand answers in front of the bellboy.

Once inside our suite, he exploded, "So will you finally tell me your real name?"

"Martins," I said quietly.

"I mean if your mother is going around spreading it all over London, surely you can be bothered to tell me," Bertram continued at volume.

"Martins," I said again. "Euphemia Martins."

"Martins?" asked Bertram. "Martins? Why on earth would you bother to conceal a name as common as that? Unless there are a Lord and Lady Martins I have never heard of?" His voice dripped sarcasm.

"I cannot understand it," I said, taking off my gloves and collapsing into a chair in a most unladylike fashion. "My mother has known how important my pseudonym is. In fact she approved of my using it. She did not wish our name to be associated with service."

"Why? It's a decent living," said Bertram.

I looked over at Bertram. He was standing legs wide, arms crossed, a fierce expression on his face. On a taller man it might have looked imposing. Dear Bertram. He had been my champion and occasionally my protector for so long. How much should I say? I felt that my mother had opened this can of worms and thus deserved whatever happened next.

"As I told you, Bertram, my father was a Vicar. My mother came from a superior social class. She eloped with him when she was very young and her family cast her off. When my father died so unexpectedly, we

202

discovered that he had had no savings and we were on the brink of destitution. My mother once again appealed to her family, but they ignored her. This is why I went into service. I saw little else that could be done, and I have a younger brother who must shortly be sent off to school." I vaguely registered that Bertram had sat down opposite me, but my mind was racing as I decided what details to give him. I had kept the truth from them all for so long I was desperate to divulge all, but instinct warned me not to do so. "My mother raised me as a lady, far above what is usual for a Vicar's daughter, and because my father observed I have a sharp mind, and was a most intelligent man himself, he gave me access to his library. He taught me far more than my mother liked." I smiled slightly. "She would always say that intelligence in a lady is as useful as having hooves."

"It would mean you didn't need shoes," said Bertram lightly.

I laughed at this. "That is exactly what I told her. I had to go to bed without supper for a week for my impertinence."

"She sounds a bit of a Tartar."

"Life has disappointed her," I said sadly. "I believe she has always tried to do her best by both Joe and I —"

"Your brother?"

I nodded, "— but she also feels that she has failed. I am very sorry to say that the love between my parents did not survive their disparity in station. My mother was ill-fitted for such a lowly life."

"Are you going to tell me you are descended from royalty?" asked Bertram, and I could see he was only half-joking.

"Not at all," I said quickly and then for the first time I lied. My paternal grandfather had been a professor at Oxford University. His wife had died young and he had kept himself very much to himself after that. He and my father corresponded at length and when I was old enough I wrote to him up until his death, some two years before my father's demise. He was a hugely intelligent man with a dry wit and huge sense of compassion. I prayed he would forgive me for what I must say next, but I needed to redirect Bertram's interest, if I was to keep my grandfather, the Earl, secret. "My father's family were in trade. They were drapers. My father had excellent manners, but he could not ever offer my mother the life she had been brought up to expect."

"So what has changed?"

"If I understood the conversation correctly she is on the verge of marrying a Bishop. I keep thinking that I must have misheard, but her comments were concise."

"A prince of the church," said Bertram, smiling. "Much more suitable. Which is your mother's family?

"But that is not the extraordinary thing," I said, diverting him away from a dangerous area. "She was having tea with an old friend, Lady Celia Blake. The woman I knew as Martha Lake."

CHAPTER
TWENTY-NINE

One last hope

"Good Gad!" said Bertram.

"I could not have put it better myself."

"We know that Harrington Blake was a friend of Wilks's. How does your mother know her?"

"You are not suggesting that my mother has anything to do with this sorry affair?"

"It seems most unlikely," said Bertram, "but then you running into her while shopping for gloves is simply extraordinary."

I bristled. "I am not lying," I said coldly.

Bertram held up his hand. "I never said that you were, but it is damnably odd. If I've understood you correctly, your mother would have had superior connections in her youth. Do you have any idea how she knows Lady Blake?"

"The Bishop is her cousin."

"So your mother had to take tea with her? I know these cleric types can be a law unto themselves . . . "

"She did say something about them being Primroses together? Some horticultural society when they were young?"

Bertram stopped lounging and sat up straight like a dog that has sniffed a postal delivery man. "She said they were Primroses? Are you sure?"

"I think so," I answered. "It was such an odd thing to say I could not forget it."

"How did Lady Blake react to your mother saying this?"

"I don't know. My attention was on my mother."

"Well this changes things a lot," said Bertram. "And I can tell you I don't like it at all."

"Can you explain why a yellow flower is causing you such distress?"

"The Primrose League included a group of women who came together to speak for politicians when paying someone to lobby for votes was outlawed. They were a highly conservative lot. Definitely the 'behind every great man is a great woman' type. Being a suffragette *and* being in the Primrose League? Not possible."

"People change," I said. "She may have revised her views."

"Has your mother?"

"Well . . . no."

"You see, that's the thing. In my experience people don't change," said Bertram. "Once they pick a political side they stick with it. It's in the blood."

"So you are saying that Lady Blake would not support the Sisterhood?"

"It seems unlikely. I mean, all things are possible, but those Primrose women were made of stern stuff."

"Hmm, it must have been when they were very young," I said, "but if Lady Blake is anything like my mother then I doubt that she will have changed her worldview so dramatically." A thought occurred to me. "Unless her marriage . . . "

"From what I could discover they are a very happy couple. No rumours. No children, but no scandal either."

"Drat," I said. "That means she was at the march for an entirely different reason."

"To kill Wilks?" asked Bertram.

"It is a bit of a stretch," I said, "but we seem to have run out of other suspects."

Bertram slapped himself on the forehead. "The letter. We have forgotten all about the letter. We must visit the boarding house."

"Surely Aggie would have burnt it," I said.

Bertram looked down his nose at me. "Most people," he said, "do not have our experience with espionage, conspiracy, and secrecy. I doubt it would have occurred to her."

"Then we shall visit Mrs Breem after breakfast tomorrow," I said. "Now we know who Martha really is, it's not as if she can run away."

"I am going to order a brandy," said Bertram suddenly. "This is all getting rather too much for me. Is there anything you would like?"

I shook my head. "No, I think it is time for me to go to bed," I said. "It has been a very long day and talking to my mother always takes it out of me."

As I left the room I heard Bertram muttering. It sounded like, "I *do* wish you wouldn't use words like that," — but that made no sense, so I readied myself for bed, and within moments of slipping between the covers I was deeply asleep.

The next morning dawned overcast, promising showers later in the day. Bertram and I sat downstairs in the hotel dining room, picking at our breakfasts and casting glances out of the window. I suspect neither of us was keen to venture abroad in such weather. The gloom without was affecting even Bertram's appetite; I had never before known him not take a second kipper. Finally, when neither of us could postpone the meal any longer, we rose and agreed to meet again in the lobby. Bertram had the task of finding us a cab and I went up to put on my hat and coat, and fetch his umbrella.

We were almost at the boarding house when the clouds gave and a light rain began to fall. The air felt chill and I huddled down further into my coat. Eyeing me, Bertram said, "I don't suppose we could . . . "

"No," I interrupted. "We do have to go through with this. Two people have died. I know little about Wilks, but Maisie was an innocent with all her life before her."

"Sometimes I hate having a sense of justice," moaned Bertram as he paid off the cabman.

The boarding house, a narrow, many-storied terrace, must once have been handsome. Now it teetered on the edge of respectability, with sparkling windows but peeling window frames. A drop of rain slid down between my coat collar and my neck. I shivered and marched smartly up to the front door. I rang the bell before Bertram could stop me.

It took a further two rings and a goodly time before we heard steps approaching the door. By this time the brim of my hat had begun to sag, and as it was one I particularly liked I was not in the best of moods when the door finally opened.

Mrs Breem stood before us in all her glory, a fox fur round her neck, paste jewels at her throat, and dressed in a tight tweed suit that she must have bought when she was younger and thinner. "Ye-es," she drawled.

"I am Aggie Phelps' cousin," I said, suddenly inspired, "and this is my brother, Edwin. We have come to collect our poor Aggie's effects."

"How do I know you are who you say you are?" asked Mrs Breem, her eyes narrowing.

"Good heavens," I replied sounded as shocked as I could. "Who would be as despicable as to pretend such a thing? I assure you I am indeed Aggie's cousin and not some vulgarly curious sightseer!" I regretted the words as soon as I had spoken them. I had given her good cause to doubt me.

"You could be from the newspapers," said Mrs Breem. "I have already had a journalist here asking questions. I sent him away with a flea in his ear, I can tell you." I fancied a martial light flickered in her eyes. This was not going well.

"We do appreciate that you will have had to re-let the room," said Bertram from behind me. "In fact I imagine that you may well be out of pocket." He smiled charmingly. "I know that Aggie would have hated such a thing to happen. She was always very precise about such things, wasn't she?"

"Well, yes." I could see her suspicions were faltering. I deviated from character and kept my mouth shut.

"Perhaps if you could work out her account," continued Bertram, "and we might have the effects? I imagine that there isn't much. Aggie would have wanted her clothes given to charity, of course," he added with a masterstroke.

Mrs Breem fairly leapt at this suggestion. "Indeed, and that is exactly what I have done — the clothes and a few other things."

"Is there nothing left?" I cried, undoing all Bertram's good work in a moment.

"She did not have much, as you would know if you were her cousin," snapped the landlady.

The edge of my hat dipped and a shower of raindrops fell on my shoe. Mrs Breem stepped back and seemed about to shut the door.

"We most want to collect her correspondence," said Bertram. "Unless the police have already taken it." He coughed in an embarrassed manner. "I believe we must confide in you. Poor Aggie had got herself involved in a few escapades that weren't quite the thing. The family don't want it getting out and casting a shadow — as it were, either over us," he paused, "or even, potentially, over where she was staying."

A guinea later and we seated in a stuffy little parlour with a small box on the table in front of us. Using extreme politeness, Bertram managed to persuade Mrs Breem to leave us alone for a few minutes while we examined the contents.

"What a deplorable woman," I said. "She must have sold all of Aggie's effects as soon as she heard she was dead!"

"Hush," whispered Bertram. "I think it unlikely she has gone further away than the other side of the door. I imagine she believed Aggie to be without relatives and was attempting to recoup her losses on rent until she could re-let the room."

"You approve?"

"Of course not. I meant only that no other meaning should be ascribed to her actions. I do not believe she was attempting to hide anything."

"Oh," I said. "It never occurred to me the landlady might be involved."

Bertram made an exasperated noise. "That is the exact opposite of what I am suggesting! I am attempting to prevent you from mistaking greed for intelligence and coming up with yet another outlandish theory."

I barely heard him. I had opened the box and was shifting through the contents. "Laundry lists! Shopping lists! A recipe for meat pudding!"

Bertram looked over my shoulder, "With capers. Interesting idea. I might suggest it to my cook."

"There's nothing here!" I cried. "No letter. Unless . . . "

"Stop thinking like Fitzroy!" snapped Bertram, pre-empting me. "It will not be in code. Besides, even if that laundry list were a code," he picked one up, glanced at it and blushed furiously, "we would not know how to decipher it."

"There is no letter from Lady Blake."

"Perhaps she had it with her when she died?" suggested Bertram.

"Fitzroy would have said."

"So the fabulous Fitzroy can now read ashes?" said Bertram vulgarly.

"Oh, I had forgotten. Do you think the firebomb was that extensive?"

"According to the papers," answered Bertram, "the train carriage burnt right down to the undercarriage."

I was about to say something about the misleading tendencies of journalists when I recalled Bertram's tragic (very short) romance with one, who had written a gossip column under the title of Lady Grey, and whose ambitions had been her downfall. "Quite," said Bertram, as if he had read my mind, "but if anything had been found I imagine he would have told you."

There was a little too much emphasis on the word "he" and the remarkable idea that Bertram might be becoming jealous of Fitzroy began to form in my mind. Before I could ask him if this were true the door opened and Mrs Breem came in. "I am afraid that is all the time I can allow you. I am a businesswoman with many claims upon my time."

"Thank you for your help," said Bertram, rising. "I believe we have seen all we need to see."

Impulsively I asked, "Did Aggie light the fire in her room on the day of the march?"

Mrs Breem's face darkened. "The girls are told by me when fires are allowed. Such a mess they make. Only in the coldest times do I permit their use."

"So she did?" I asked eagerly.

"Yes. I remember because it was quite out of character for her. She was never one to flout rules in the general way of things. A quiet respectable woman, I always thought. Well, we all know different now, don't we? The room still smells of smoke despite the expense of extra cleaning."

Silently Bertram handed her a few more coins, although this time I could see there was nothing more than silver in them. Mrs Breem, offended but also unwilling to let go of an extra penny, showed us to the door and told us not to come back.

We stood on the doorstep in the rain. "She burnt it," I said miserably.

"It seems likely," said Bertram. "I am sorry, Euphemia. I think this must be the end of it. We have nowhere else left to look."

CHAPTER
THIRTY

Bertram plays poker

Seated once more in the back of a cab, I felt almost as low as I had upon my father's own sudden demise. I gave a big sigh. Bertram laid his hand lightly on mine. "We have done everything we could."

"I still feel that I have failed," I said sadly.

"Even the great Fitzroy was stumped by this one," said Bertram lightly.

"Yes, but he was not in the cell when Maisie was killed. I feel responsible. How could I not have noticed?"

"You had had a difficult and trying day," said Bertram. "I do not doubt you were exhausted. Besides what reason did you have to think she was in danger."

I turned my head to face him, blinking back tears. "She was so young, Bertram, and she was so scared. I should have tried harder to get her to talk to me."

"I am sure you did all you could."

"I wish I thought so," I replied. "I fear my guilt over her death will always weigh heavily on me."

"That is ridiculous," said Bertram. "The guilt lies with the killer."

"I am not sure emotions can be over-ruled by rationality. I do know that I am not wholly to blame, but I was a participant in the actions around her death. If I had played my part differently . . . "

Bertram rapped on the cab with his cane. Then he redirected us to the Blake's house.

"What on earth are you doing?"

"Have I ever told you, Euphemia, that I am rather good at poker? I don't play very much because generally I find gambling somewhat of a bore. Or at least the people who play it are, but in the gentleman's clubs in town I am known as 'Bluffing Bertie.'"

"No," I said shocked.

"No, well, but I should be," said Bertram. "I am remarkably good at bluffing at cards." I must have looked doubtful. In my limited experience Bertram was extremely prone to blushing. "It is all in the mind set," he said. "Once one thinks oneself into the game. It is straightforward. Players have many different strategies. I run through the number of fish I know."

"Fish?" I said bewildered.

"Yes, I name all the freshwater ones I can think of first and then I move on to the sea ones. If I have to continue I run through the alphabet naming fruit. In my head of course."

"You mean you concentrate on not thinking about the bluff?" I said as understanding dawned. Bertram nodded eagerly. "But how does this help us?"

"I say," said Bertram, "we visit the Blakes. We let Lady Blake know we have made the acquaintance of Mrs Breem and that we know all."

"But we don't know anything. We only suspect."

"That's the bluff."

"But we have no idea why Lady Blake would have done this!" I protested. "If indeed she did."

"It will be love, money, fear of scandal, or all three," said Bertram. "Perhaps she was having an affair with Wilks and he threatened to leave her."

"Or was blackmailing her over it?" I said. "There are a thousand and one reasons."

"That's why we are going to bluff," said Bertram. "We are going to make her think we know."

"This is a very adventurous plan for you," I said. "Even I am daunted."

"I am not totally averse to risk, you know," said Bertram, looking hurt. "Besides, you are so upset by this damn business and Fitzroy has swanned off, abandoning you."

"So you are going to fix what Fitzroy could not?" I said, a smile playing on my lips.

"Yes, I damn well am!" said Bertram.

I felt this plan was the height of foolishness, but I did not have the heart to stop him. Bertram had his pride like any other man. I only hoped he could pull it off.

When the cab drew up outside the Blakes' London residence I half expected sense to have taken up its rightful place in Bertram's brains once more, but it appeared not. He paid the cabman and helped me out. "What if they are not in?"

"It is luncheon time. If she is not at home then I shall persuade the butler to tell us where she is engaged and we will go and wait for her," said Bertram and strode up to the front door.

Our bearing, accents, and visiting cards ensured the butler admitted us. However, he set us to wait in a side room as luncheon was about to be served. "I fear you will have to wait, sir, madam. Unless you would like to call later in the day?" he said hopefully.

"I am afraid our business with Lady Blake is of some urgency," said Bertram.

"In that case I shall see if some tea and fruit can be sent up to you," said the butler bowing slightly. "Unless you would prefer sherry?"

I could see from Bertram's face he was on the verge of asking for a swift brandy, but he pulled himself back from the brink and declined for both of us.

We were in a small morning room that overlooked the street. On a good day doubtless the large windows made it a very pleasant room. The furniture, much padded, was of blue and white and in brighter light might have been quite cheering. However, today it was cold and somehow sad. The fire had not been lit and the empty hearth reminded me of a black abyss. I said as much to Bertram and he told me to stop daydreaming. The door opened, but instead of the butler, a well-dressed, middle-aged man with iron grey hair and a serious demeanour entered.

"I am Harrington Blake," he announced. "I hear you wish to see my wife? I am afraid, Mr Stapleford, Miss St John, your names are quite unknown to me."

"Indeed," said Bertram. "We are most sorry to disturb you, but our business concerns only your wife."

"When a strange man demands to see his wife might a husband not enquire the reason why?"

"My mother, Mrs Martins, is engaged to your wife's cousin," I said desperately. "Mr Stapleford is merely escorting me."

"Which one?"

At this point I realised that my mother had not told me her beau's name. "The Bishop," I said hoping that the Blake family were not generally ecumenically minded.

"Oh, Larry," said Sir Harrington. "I had heard something of that. Still, it is a very strange time to call, young lady."

"The matter is urgent," piped up Bertram.

"Very well," said Sir Harrington, "I shall send for my wife to join us, but I will remain. My wife has been out of sorts of late. She has recently returned from a short period of convalescence, but it seems to have done little to restore her."

Bertram and I exchanged glances. Did her husband really not know where she had been?

Sir Harrington rang for the butler, who appeared with a tea tray which he set down and then went to find Lady Blake.

The lady entered the room, glancing from Bertram to I and I thought I saw a flash of fear, but it was quickly covered as she swept in to kiss me on both cheeks. "Euphemia, how charming! Your mother did not tell me that you were going to call on us."

"We have been so see Mrs Breem," said Bertram.

Lady Blake paled.

"She allowed us to look through Aggie Phelps' effects," I said gently. "To see her letters."

Lady Blake sank down onto a chair. Her husband hurried to her side. "My dear, do you feel unwell? Shall I send for a doctor?"

"Tea," said Lady Blake, "some tea, Harry."

Her husband hurriedly poured her a cup and passed it to her. Lady Blake took one sip and pulled a face. "I never take sugar with China tea. You should know that by now."

And then I knew. I knew she had killed Maisie, but how on earth was it ever to be proved?

Harrington Blake turned on us. "I don't know what you are about, but you have distressed my wife. I must ask you to leave this house immediately."

I ignored him. "Did Maisie see something?" I asked. "Was it you that set the bomb. Is that why she had to die?"

"Die? Bomb? What are you blathering about?" demanded Blake.

"And Aggie, did she have any idea she would die? Did she think it was some kind of test? Whatever Wilks did to you, you killed two innocent women. What could be worth such evil?"

"And you tried to put the blame on the suffragettes," said Bertram.

Lady Blake gave a low moan and her cup tipped out of her hand. Sir Harrington knelt beside her. "My dear, you are unwell. You must go upstairs and rest. I will deal with these people."

Lady Blake brought her mouth close to her husband's ear and whispered something. Harrington went white. He helped his wife to her feet. "Go," he said. "I will arrange matters."

Lady Blake tottered to the door. She had aged before our very eyes. She shut the door carefully behind her without looking back. "Now," said Sir Harrington Blake turning to us, "I don't know what you think you know, but I should warn you I am a man of significance in this country and I will not stand to see my wife slandered in any way whatsoever."

"There are deaths to be accounted for, Sir Harrington," said Bertram. "I gather from your wife's reaction and yours that she did what she did to protect you. You are, as you say, a man of significance. A rising star in political circles, so I am told. And rising stars can afford no scandal."

"Hah!" said Blake, "and this coming from a man related to Richard Stapleford, a blackguard if ever there was one."

"You said you did not know me," said Bertram.

"One does not *know* persons of such a background. As for you, Miss Martins, I would have thought you had quite enough scandal in your own personal history without adding to it. I warn you both, any allegations you dare to make will be disproved utterly by the best lawyers in the country. You will both be ruined."

"You are very loyal to her, sir," I said, "but you cannot condone what she has done."

220

Blake hesitated then, and I saw that although he now suspected, he did not know the full extent of his wife's activities.

"There was a young girl called Maisie in the cell with your wife and myself," I began, but at that moment we were all distracted by a shadow falling past the window.

"Good God! Was that a body?" said Bertram rushing to the window. And then the screaming outside began.

Final Correspondence

Sir Harrington Blake announced in the newspapers his decision to retire from public life to focus on his recent purchase of a railway line. In this the article salaciously added he would be joined by his natural son, whom two weeks after his wife's unfortunate accident he named as his heir.

Fitzroy sent me a brief note with a smudged foreign postmark. It read:

All sorted then? F
P.S. I hear you look well in red.

Of course, I immediately burnt his note.

And, lastly, my mother wrote to say that despite "occurrences" she remained engaged to her Bishop and would be married in the New Year. When, she added, she expected me to join her and little Joe, and live at the Bishop's Palace.

To be continued . . .

Other titles published by Ulverscroft:

WILD CHAMBER

Christopher Fowler

Near London Bridge Station, members of the Met's Peculiar Crimes Unit race to catch a killer. In the dark and the rain, they unwittingly cause a bizarre accident — one that will have repercussions for them all . . . One year later, a smartly dressed woman is found strangled in a locked private London garden. The dog she was walking has disappeared, her husband is missing, and a nanny has vanished too — so far, so typical a case for Bryant and May. As Bryant delves into the arcane history of London's extraordinary parks and gardens — its "wild chambers" — May and the rest of the team become mired in a national scandal. It seems likely that the killer is preparing to strike again, and if the city's open spaces aren't safe, then surely they must be closed . . .

DATE WITH MALICE

Julia Chapman

When Mrs Shepherd arrives at the Dales Detective Agency on a December morning, quite convinced that someone is trying to kill her, Samson O'Brien dismisses her fears as the ramblings of a confused elderly lady. But after a series of disturbing incidents at Fellside Court retirement home, he begins to wonder if there is something to her claims after all. Soon Samson is thrown into a complex investigation — one that will require him to regain the trust of the Dales community he turned his back on so long ago. Faced with no choice, he enlists the help of a local — the tempestuous Delilah Metcalfe. Against the backdrop of a Yorkshire winter, they must work together once again if they are to uncover the malevolence threatening the elderly residents of Bruncliffe . . .